Acclaim for *The House of Eyes*, the first Connie Carew Mystery . . .

'Elliott . . . has a light touch and there's humour everywhere in this book . . . It's funny, exciting, well-written and has a ᴐper plot and structure . . . This is a delightful book which ᴐ enjoyed enormously.' *Adèle Geras on An Awfully Big Blog ᴐventure*

ᴠas drawn in from the very beginning and read it in two ᴐ ings. I think this series will be a huge hit. I'm recommending it ᴐ my nine-year-old to read.' *Miss Chapter's Reviews*

ᴐ ᴐe of the most enjoyable books I've read this year. I'd love ᴐᴐre of her adventures.' *GoodReads*

ᴐ action-packed read which . . . builds to a stunning reveal. Hugely excited for more Connie Carew mysteries.'
ᴐ *on Moon Lane*

ᴐ always, Patricia Elliott brings her time period to life ᴠ ᴐderfully well in this historical mystery set against a ᴐ ᴐdrop of suffragettes, séances and a mystery cousin who m ᴐave returned from the dead . . . Connie Carew has to ᴐᴐ ᴐe of the best detectives in MG today. I'd really looking ᴐ ᴐ rd to more of her adventures.' *YA YeahYeah*

ᴐᴐᴐs ᴐ new series off to a great start. Good period detail and lang ᴐ ᴐge, ᴠell-depicted characters. I'm looking forward to more. *Parenᴐ in Touch*

And so, without further ado, we present . . .

Also by Patricia Elliott

The Ice Boy
Winner of the Fidler Award 2001; shortlisted for the Branford Boase Award 2003 and the West Sussex Award

Murkmere
Longlisted for the Guardian Children's Fiction Award 2004 and shortlisted for the Calderdale Award 2005

Ambergate

The Night Walker
Shortlisted for the Wirral Paperback of the Year

Pimpernelles: The Pale Assassin

Pimpernelles: The Traitor's Smile

A Connie Carew Mystery: The House of Eyes

For older readers …
The Devil in the Corner

Patricia Elliott

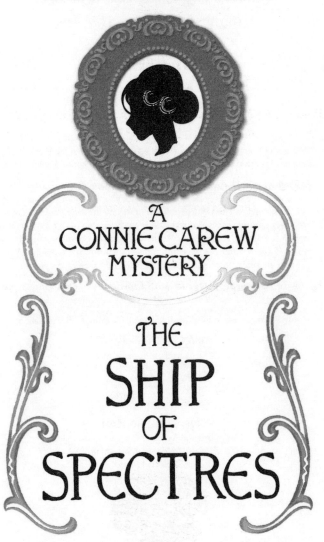

A
CONNIE CAREW
MYSTERY

THE
SHIP
OF
SPECTRES

Hodder
Children's
Books

With thanks to Janey Blanchflower,
for introducing me to the delights of the
Marine Bookshop in Harwich

HODDER CHILDREN'S BOOKS

First published in Great Britain in 2016 by Hodder Children's Books

1 3 5 7 9 10 8 6 4 2

A Catalogue record for this book is available from the British Library

ISBN 978 1 444 92471 8

Hodder Children's Books
An imprint of Hachette Children's Group
Part of Hodder and Stoughton
Carmelite House
50 Victoria Embankment
London EC4Y 0DZ

An Hachette UK Company
www.hachette.co.uk

For Guillemette, with love

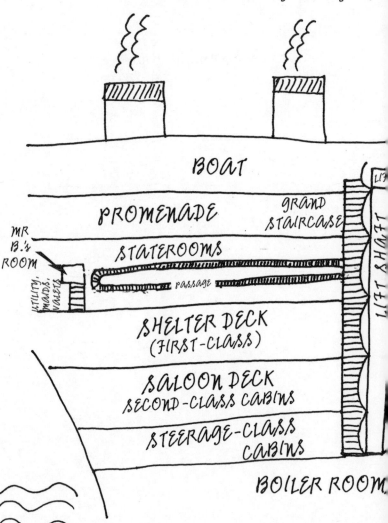

plan of HMS Princess May on Day 1 of h

BOAT

PROMENADE

GRAND STAIRCASE

LIFT

LIFT SHAFT

MR B.'s ROOM

STATEROOMS

passage

UTILITY, MAIDS, VALETS

SHELTER DECK
(FIRST-CLASS)

SALOON DECK
SECOND-CLASS CABINS

STEERAGE-CLASS
CABINS

BOILER ROOM

DECK

DECK   FIRST-CLASS LOUNGE
GYMNASIUM. ETC.

BRIDGE DECK

FIRST CLASS CABINS

TEA LOUNGE
LIBRARY
GENTLEMEN'S SMOKING ROOM ETC.

FIRST-CLASS DINING SALOON   + LOUNGE
SECOND-CLASS
READING + WRITING ROOM   ETC.
GAMES GALLERY

...INING SALOON + LOUNGE   BALLROOM

(ADDED LATER)

From an early notebook of Miss Constance Carew, Anthropologist

Among those on board HMS Princess May –
maiden voyage, August 1909:

Mr Waldo Bamberger, owner of Shining Seas
shipping line
Mr Louie Leblank, entertainment manager
Madame Radmilla Oblomov, prima ballerina with
the Ballets Russes
Mrs Cornelia Cartmell, owner of hotel chain
Master Elmer Cartmell, her son
Mrs Muriel Pope, Mrs Cartmell's companion
Mr Hiram Fink, rich financier
Mr 'Biffer' Smith, journalist
Miss Verina Vane, actress
Miss Dolores Devine, actress
Miss Ida Fairbanks, heiress
Mr Arthur Harker, music student
Miss Constance Clementine Carew

1

On a calm Sunday afternoon at the end of August 1909, a young girl of about twelve stood on the boat deck of the new luxury steamship, HMS *Princess May*, and watched the other first-class passengers embark in the sunshine. Her name was Constance Clementine Carew and she was about to set sail to New York on the voyage of a lifetime.

Her two aunts had come from London to the Southampton docks to see the small party off: Connie, her cousin Ida and Ida's fiancé, Arthur. The three of them were travelling first-class at the invitation of the ship's owner, for Arthur was to play the piano in the evenings to entertain the diners.

'Take care, my darling,' fey Aunt Sylvie had hissed in her ear, as Connie stepped on to the gangway. 'I see danger ahead!'

But Connie was used to Aunt Sylvie's premonitions.

Leading the way, with Ida and Arthur behind her, she looked up at the dazzling sides of the *Princess May* curving before her in the sun and smiled.

What could possibly go wrong?

Ida wanted to inspect their cabins straight away and Arthur, who did everything his beautiful fiancée wanted, as if he still couldn't believe his luck, followed obediently behind, laden with hat boxes.

Connie had decided to stay outside; everything was much too interesting to miss. She went as high as she possibly could, to the boat deck, using one of the thrilling glass lifts. She was alone, apart from a large seagull perched near her, observing the scene below with a look of displeasure. From where Connie stood looking down, the embarking first-class passengers were a line of bobbing heads in enormous hats advancing along the gangway.

On the crowded dock, press photographers were taking pictures of two laughing girls with lipsticked mouths. Camera bulbs popped and puffs of white smoke drifted up to the blue sky.

Ida, in great excitement, had already pointed them out to Connie as the aspiring young actresses, Dolores Devine and Verina Vane. Ida loved glamour because she had known only squalor in her previous life at the orphanage; she had been excited to learn that the actresses would also be among Mr Bamberger's special guests.

Next, the press caught sight of a tall man in a city suit, who was hurrying to the gangway with a bent head, as if he wanted to escape notice.

'Mr Fink! What's going on on the New York stock exchange? Are you going to tell us the best investments?'

Mr Fink brushed the journalists out of his way impatiently and stepped on to the gangway. Behind him the band blasted out 'Rule Britannia', while scurrying stewards in their summer whites encouraged passengers to board, porters rushed through the crowds with trolleys piled with luggage, and seagulls cackled overhead.

Then there was a sudden commotion, adding to the noise. Mr Waldo Bamberger himself, owner of the Shining Seas shipping line, had arrived on the dock and was looking up in an appraising way at his magnificent new ship. The journalists left Mr Fink and rushed over to him in a hectic bunch.

For several months past, Mr Bamberger had appeared in the newspaper pictures that had accompanied stories about the launch of the *Princess May*: a short, stocky man, with a fleshy face, clever eyes and a commanding presence. In spite of his somewhat rotund shape there was something neat and dapper about him.

He had been to see Arthur at the house in South Kensington several times to discuss the music that Arthur was to play during dinner on board ship. At these visits Mr Bamberger had made the acquaintance of Connie, and they had enjoyed sensible and interesting conversations over Cook's Victoria sponge cake. By now they were firm friends.

Connie waved at him, leaning over the wooden deck rail. 'Hello, Mr Bamberger!' she shouted, but he didn't hear.

The reporters began to fire out questions as the band stopped for a moment. The voices came up clearly on the warm, still air.

'Mr Bamberger! They say that the *Princess May* will be the fastest ship on water! Can you beat the great *Mauretania* and win the Blue Riband?'

'Mr Bamberger! How many celebrity guests do you have on board?'

'Mr Bamberger! Is it true that you've given exclusive coverage of the voyage itself to Biffer Smith?'

Mr Bamberger nodded briefly and the journalist who had asked looked mortified. His editor would not be pleased to hear that a rival newspaper had been awarded one of the best stories of the summer.

'Now gentlemen, please!' Mr Bamberger held up his hands in good-humoured protest. 'You're blocking the way! My guests can't embark.'

All the same, another journalist butted in aggressively. 'Is it true that a mechanic fell during the building of the ship and his body was never recovered, Mr Bamberger?'

The crowd fell silent. Connie craned over the rail as Mr Bamberger turned back. She could see that he was disconcerted. He forgot to greet a very important-looking personage as she swept up to the gangway, her elderly companion and a boy in tow.

'Stale news!' said Mr Bamberger evenly. 'Accidents occur during ship building. Now, if you will excuse me . . .' And with that he strode up the gangway.

Back on the dock two passengers had caught Connie's eye. A man pushing a bath chair in which sat an old woman wrapped in a travelling rug, a hat and veil covering her face. They were helped on to the first-class gangway by a steward.

A little while later, Connie heard a young, enthusiastic voice say 'Hiya!' behind her. When she looked round, a boy was almost breathing down her neck, his eyes shining with eagerness. The seagull flew off in disgust.

'Begging your pardon, miss, but I guess we're the only young ones among Mr Bamberger's guests, so I thought I'd make your acquaintance.' He had an American accent and his voice squeaked up and down alarmingly. 'Name's Elmer *Cartmell*.' The boy put extra emphasis on his surname as if Connie should have heard of it.

'Constance Clementine Carew,' said Connie politely.

He was older than her, thirteen perhaps, but not a prepossessing sight: spotty chin, hair slicked back in a quiff and overdressed, in a topcoat and knickerbockers. It made Connie feel hot to look at him, though she was only wearing her linen sailor dress. His hand when she shook it was limp and slightly damp. But he was beaming at her expectantly, as if he anticipated their becoming the greatest of friends.

'I saw you embarking,' said Connie.

He nodded vigorously and beamed some more.

'You were with – your mother?'

'My marm, yeah. She owns hotels in New York and Boston. They're very grand hotels and she's very famous. She wants to open her next one in

London. She's English but my pop's American. He's famous, too.'

'I haven't heard of them but then I've never been to America,' said Connie.

Elmer whistled. 'Boy! Never been to the US of A?' He studied her as he might some extraordinary specimen.

'Most English girls my age haven't,' said Connie defensively. 'But when I grow up I mean to travel lots. I'm going to be an anthropologist.'

Elmer let out a chortle. 'A what?'

'An anthropologist. It's a sort of scientist, only instead of studying chemicals and things, they study peoples. The peoples of the world. I've started already, actually.'

Elmer looked worried.

'Gee whiz! Does that mean you'll study me?'

'It might do,' said Connie airily. 'If you're interesting enough.'

He shook his head and his quiff quivered. 'It's my mother you should study,' he blurted out, his voice squeakier than ever. 'She's a case right on her own.'

Connie looked at him carefully. 'It doesn't sound as if you like her very much.'

Elmer kicked the side of the deck with his

correspondent shoe, blinking rapidly. 'What's *your* marm like?'

'She's dead. My father, too. I live with my two aunts and my cousin. Ida's on this voyage with me. So's her fiancé, Arthur. He's going to play the piano at dinner.'

'Lolla palooza! Excellent!'

'Is your father on board?'

His face changed and he shook his head. 'My marm and pop don't live together any more. But anyhow he owns a rival shipping company, the Poseidon line. I guess my marm's travelling on the *Princess May* to pay him back!'

'Has he given you your own ship yet?' asked Connie. 'He must have lots to spare.'

'Only a sailboat.'

Still, to have your own sailing boat sounded pretty satisfactory to Connie. But Elmer was gazing down at the dock despondently and the conversation seemed to have faltered to an end.

'I'd better go and find my cousin and her fiancé,' Connie said. 'I'm meant to be looking after them.'

Elmer switched on a smile again. 'Sure thing, Miss Constance. It's been real swell meeting you.'

The first-class passenger cabins were mostly on the bridge deck, two levels down, so it was a good excuse to use the lift again. Connie would have liked to have flown up and down in it some more, but other passengers entered at the promenade deck and looked at her disapprovingly, as if they thought children should be confined in their cabins well out of the way until the ship reached New York.

Connie found herself in a gleaming passage, with the cabin numbers in brass on the doors. The cabins in this part of the ship were so grand that they were called 'staterooms', as if the occupants were very important indeed.

Her feet in the soft-soled deck shoes, bought for her by Aunt Dorothea for the voyage, squeaked on the polished floor. The electrical lights were on, glowing from little bulbs along the walls, and the air smelled of luxury, of furniture wax, mahogony fittings and new paint.

Their stateroom was filled with Ida's cruise wear, which she had not yet put away, and her new shipboard trunks, which took up much of the floor space. It was fortunate that it was large, much larger than Connie expected, and wonderfully luxurious.

Connie took off her boater with relief and threw it on the floor: it always pinched her forehead. Trying to avoid treading on Ida's clothes, she darted round to examine everything: a porcelain basin with brass taps out of which flowed hot and cold water, a dressing-table with a vase of fresh flowers reflected in its mirror, a desk with a leather box of stationery stamped HMS *Princess May* and a new notebook lying beside it, just as if it was meant for her.

The porthole was actually a real window with curtains. Connie peered through but couldn't see much except blue August sky.

'Where do I sleep?' she asked, looking around a little plaintively. Ida's bed had a mahogany bedhead with a gilt surround but it was certainly not meant for two.

Arthur was sitting on the end of Ida's bed, watching Ida toss her cruise wear out of her trunks. He sprang up in answer to Connie's question and pulled down part of the panelled wall with a long arm. Only it wasn't the wall: it was a cleverly disguised bunk bed that could be pushed up out of the way during the day. It was neatly made already, with embroidered linen sheets and cream wool blankets.

Connie bounced on it several times to her satisfaction and then Arthur pushed it up again.

'There's a grand piano for me to play in the dining saloon, Connie! I've had a go on it already.' He looked dazzled. 'There's bound to be one in the ballroom, too!'

Ida gave an exhausted sigh and collapsed on her bed, crushing her new clothes. 'Them press photographers down on the dock they didn't half pester me. Kept asking me about me fortune. As if I'd let on!' She propped herself on her elbows and gazed at them both, her eyes shining. 'But this is luxury, eh? Look at me, in all this splendour! Me, a girl from an orphanage in Hammersmith!'

In times of excitement or stress, Ida was liable to forget she had been taught to speak 'proper' by Aunt Dorothea, as befitted a young lady who had recently been reclaimed by her family and, as a result, inherited a considerable amount of money.

'You're more than that, Ida,' said Arthur fondly. 'You always have been. And now you're my fiancée too!'

'You're not going to kiss, are you?' said Connie in disgust. It seemed to be their favourite occupation at the moment. 'First of all, you can tell me what *that* is – it's not one of Ida's.' She pointed to a round vanity case of dark green leather sitting in the corner.

Ida shook her head. 'That was with our luggage by mistake. I should give it to the steward.'

'I'll have a look,' said Connie. 'Maybe there's a label on it.'

There was no clue on the outside. As she turned it to examine it properly, her fingers caught in the catch and the lid sprang open. Inside there were little compartments covered in flesh-coloured silk, filled with what looked like wax crayons, and nestling in pleated satin in the lid was a large mirror, which could be pulled out on metal arms. How very intriguing.

'Oh, Connie!' said Arthur. 'You shouldn't look in other people's possessions.'

'I didn't mean to,' protested Connie. 'But now I can't help it, can I?'

'Isn't it darling?' said Ida, pulling out the mirror and peering at herself.

Arthur couldn't resist coming over to look too. 'It's stage make-up,' he announced. He knew about such things, having worked in his holidays from the Royal College of Music playing the piano for the rehearsals of various artistic companies.

Connie shut the case again, then lifted it up on a sudden inspiration. Stuck to the bottom was a Shining Seas label that said *St. rm. 55.*

She jumped up. 'I'll take it.'

Number 55 was further along the passage and the bath chair she had seen earlier, now empty of its occupant, was sitting outside the door. Connie hesitated, then knocked.

'*Nyet!* No!' shouted a voice from inside. It sounded female and dauntingly fierce.

The door opened and the man she had seen pushing the chair poked his head out. He looked grey and harrassed. He frowned at Connie. 'It's all right, Radmilla, it's not press,' he called over his shoulder. Then he caught sight of the case and his face cleared.

'This was delivered to our stateroom by mistake,' explained Connie. 'I think it belongs to your wife.'

'She's been such trouble since she discovered it missing,' said the man. 'I'm so grateful to you.' He took it from Connie and whispered, 'She's terrified of the press realising she's on board. She'll be better once the ship leaves Southampton.' He winked at her, looking suddenly cheerful. 'I'm only her dresser, you know – not important enough for a free passage!'

Fancy having someone especially to dress you!

13

But then an old woman might need help with fastening her clothes. As Connie was thinking that, a face popped up behind the man and it wasn't old at all: it was scarcely lined and dazzlingly attractive, with high cheekbones and huge eyes rimmed in black.

Connie gazed at it, speechless. Was this who had been hiding under the rug? From the press? That meant she must be famous, too, like everyone else on the *Princess May*, it seemed.

Before she could ask any questions, the beautiful face had disappeared and the man had disappeared too, giving her a brief nod of thanks and another wink as he shut the door.

As Connie made her way back to her stateroom, an electrical bell shrilled through the passage. A voice announced that the *Princess May* was about to depart on her maiden voyage and that all those who weren't passengers should leave at once. Then somewhere deep below a rumble started up.

The most exciting trip of Connie's life so far was beginning!

2

They had steamed down Southampton Water and passed the Isle of Wight, leaving the squawking gulls far behind. Now there was nothing around the *Princess May* but flat sea, rolling out to the horizon on all sides, with only the occasional tiniest curl of white to disturb it.

An electrical bell sounded again, summoning passengers to safety drill.

Connie, Ida and Arthur climbed the sweeping staircase to the first-class lounge, which was a level higher, on the promenade deck.

'It's all so big, I'll never find me way around!' said Ida. 'It's much worse than being in Harrods!'

'I'll draw you a map,' offered Connie. By now she had more or less mastered the layout of the ship and indeed throughly explored their own deck, the bridge deck.

Their passage contained the staterooms for Mr Bamberger's special guests and other first-class passengers. Mr Bamberger's own stateroom was at the far end, where the passage looped round and ran back down until it reached the landing with the lift. On this parallel side there weren't any staterooms but several closed doors.

The first three were marked *Utility*, *Stewards*, *Bellboys*. There was noise coming from the latter two and Connie had thought it wisest not to investigate further.

But beyond them lay a mysterious row of doors with labels pinned to them, such as *Countess of Yarborough's maid* and *Mr Fink's valet*, written neatly in black ink. All was silent behind them and they were unlocked. When Connie peered in, she had discovered not cabins but intriguing little pantries equipped with sinks and ironing-boards, racks of shoe polish and shelves piled with teacups and saucers.

The first-class lounge, when she led Ida and Arthur there for the safety drill, was enormous and opulent, with plaster panels on the walls decorated with flowers and exotic birds. It was filled with natural daylight from an ornate skylight which took up a large part of the ceiling.

They sat at one of the little round tables and stared

at each other in wonder, trying to hide smiles of glee and look as if they travelled first-class all the time.

'Fancy!' said Ida. 'Here we are, sitting in the lap of luxury and all because of you, Arthur!' She stretched back in the armchair. 'I couldn't half do with a cup of tea, though!'

'Tea, madam?' said a voice. A man bent over her solicitously. He was highly polished from the top of his head to his dazzling patent leather shoes. His black hair gleamed so smoothly it might have been painted on to his scalp. Beneath it his face was unnaturally white and scored with deep lines.

'Let me introduce myself.' His voice, with its soft accent, was like warm oil. 'Louie Leblank, Mr Bamberger's entertainment manager.' He snapped his fingers at a passing steward. 'Tea for three –' he looked at Connie '– and a plate of cookies for the kiddo.'

Connie disliked being called 'kiddo' intensely but she was hungry.

Louie Leblank gave them a bow and hurried off to look after more passengers. The lounge was filling up.

While Ida and Arthur gazed adoringly into each other's eyes over their teacups, Connie munched through the cookies – which turned out to be delicious little biscuits – and watched the other first-class

17

passengers come in.

She recognised the financier, Hiram Fink, who came in with his briefcase, without looking at anyone else, and sat by himself. He immediately retrieved some papers and began studying them. Connie could see his frown from where she sat.

She recognised at once the high cheekbones and exotic looks of the woman she had seen earlier. The woman took a table in a corner, well out of the light.

'Look! There's stateroom fifty-five!' hissed Connie.

'What?' With an effort Arthur wrenched his eyes away from Ida's sky blue ones.

'The woman who owns the vanity case!' said Connie impatiently.

Arthur's jaw dropped. He stared. 'That, Connie, is Radmilla Oblomov, prima ballerina with the great Diaghilev's company, the Ballets Russes!'

It meant nothing to either Connie or Ida, but Arthur had turned pink.

'I wonder if I shall have a chance to play for her while she dances. What an honour that would be!' He gazed longingly across the room.

'Miss Constance!'

It was Elmer Cartmell again, this time accompanied by the woman Connie had seen embarking with him, who must be his mother. Mrs Cartmell was well-upholstered and immaculately coiffed, and smelled of eau de Cologne, efficiency and wealth. She was dressed in the palest lavender silk, which spoke to anyone who knew about such things, of perfect taste.

Mrs Cartmell's glance swept disparagingly over Connie, whose own hair had long escaped its ringlets and whose sailor dress was now covered in crumbs.

'Is this the girl you told me about, Elmer?'

Elmer blinked nervously. 'Yes, Marmee,' he said, and his voice squeaked. 'Miss Constance Clementine Carew.'

Connie stood up and held out her hand. 'You may call me Connie.'

Mrs Cartmell ignored her hand; Connie was certain that her lip even curled a little in disdain before she turned away to survey Ida and Arthur with sharp eyes.

Ida gave her sweet smile and rose languidly. 'Miss Ida Fairbanks. Pleased to meet you, I'm sure.'

Mrs Cartmell's eyes widened as she took in first Ida's name – which had been well known to London society that summer – then her undoubted beauty and finally her dress, which surely had been designed by Monsieur Paul Poiret, the celebrated French couturier himself, with its new high waist and slim skirt.

'What a pleasure to meet you, Miss Fairbanks,' she said, a little breathlessly. 'Of course, I've read a great deal about you . . .' In the background, Elmer recovered, basking in the reflected glory of his new friend's friend.

'The press! Don't believe a word they say!' said Ida to Mrs Cartmell. She winked. 'Great big fibbers, all of 'em!'

'Is it true that you are engaged, Miss Fairbanks?' Mrs Cartmell said, in an intimate tone, 'And your fiancé is travelling with us, I gather from the newspapers.' She looked around. 'You have a chaperone on board, I presume?'

Connie stepped forward. 'It's me.'

'Surely not? You are far too young!'

'But Connie always looks after me and Arthur,' said Ida.

'Arthur?'

Arthur sprang up. 'Arthur Harker. How do you do?'

Arthur's appearance was elegant, though a little shabby, and his manners were always faultless, thought Connie proudly; he had been her dearly loved best friend before they had even met Ida.

'We aren't marrying for at least a year,' said Ida blithely. 'Arthur is still a student, you see.'

'A student?' Mrs Cartmell looked him up and down and her lip seemed to curl a little more. 'Oh, dear.'

Elmer bit his lip and looked nervously at Connie.

'A music student,' said Ida quickly, as if that made all the difference.

Mrs Cartmell tried to give a little laugh, but it didn't alter her face. 'Well, I don't suppose it matters that he'll be penniless, married to you, Miss Fairbanks!'

'He won't be penniless,' Connie said indignantly. She was determined to make Mrs Cartmell see Arthur's worth. 'Arthur is a genius at playing the piano. Soon the whole world will recognise it, just as Mr Bamberger's done!'

A large hand came to rest on her shoulder and a large voice spoke in her ear. 'And who is taking my name in vain? Ah, it's you, Connie!'

'Hello, Mr Bamberger. Your ship is A1!'

'That's reassuring to hear, Connie. I hope you're making yourself at home.'

'Home? It's like a giant hotel!'

'It must be the largest luxury liner on water!' said Ida, wide-eyed.

Mr Bamberger shook his head, smiling at the group. 'They'll be building one that's real titanic next!' He caught Mrs Cartmell's steely eye with reluctance.

'You're comfortable, Cornelia? I know what a stickler you are for high standards.'

'Indeed!' said Mrs Cartmell. 'There are one or two things in my room that could be improved upon for future voyages. If I might have a word, Waldo?'

Mr Bamberger gestured with relief at a steward, who was holding his hand up for silence. 'Later, Cornelia. I believe we are about to start the drill.'

'But perhaps you could tell me –' said Mrs Cartmell, in a deceptively flirtatious tone, cocking her head to one side '– what that man is doing on board this ship?' She gestured at Leblank, who was bustling about, giving out the life-preserver vests. 'He was working for my husband until recently! Have you stolen him, Waldo?'

'Not at all,' said Mr Bamberger mildly. 'Your husband was about to make him redundant. He told him he was too old for the job. I thought I would give him a second chance.'

Mrs Cartmell's immaculate eyebrows rose, but she made no comment. She was persuaded to sit down with Elmer and they were given their life-preservers. Mrs Cartmell accepted hers graciously and Mr Bamberger took the opportunity to hurry away.

'Where is Mrs Pope?' she grumbled, to no one in

particular, as instructions began to boom through a megaphone. 'I never should have taken her on!'

She didn't speak to Elmer, except to tell him off for tying his tapes in knots. He looked crestfallen and Connie couldn't help feeling sorry for him.

The life-preservers were canvas vests, with long pockets inserted with cork, and fastened at the sides with tapes. Ida, Arthur and Connie put theirs on and Connie giggled. How peculiar they all looked, like overgrown babies in bibs!

'There was a dreadful accident on that White Star liner in January,' said Cornelia Cartmell snappishly, from the neighbouring table. 'One shouldn't be flippant. The ship collided with another one and sank!'

'But thanks to the emergency wireless signal no lives were lost,' said Louie Leblank smoothly, appearing from nowhere at just the right moment, as he always seemed to do. 'Let me assure you, we have Signor Marconi's new wireless telegraphy on the *Princess May*.'

He recognised Mrs Cartmell and his face registered embarrassment. A little colour came into his pale cheeks. Then almost as quickly he was in control of himself.

'How delightful to see you again, madam. I saw your name on Mr Bamberger's list, of course, and was looking forward to our reacquaintance.'

'I doubt that,' said Cornelia Cartmell, while next to her Connie noticed Elmer scowling from his chair. 'I gather you have jumped ship!'

Louie Leblank was spared a reply, for at that moment an elderly woman came haltingly up to Mrs Cartmell's table.

She had a slight stoop but there was also something ungainly about her. Her long skirt hung drably and her blouse was pinned with a tarnished brooch. Her dust-coloured hair, streaked with grey, was busy escaping its old-fashioned bun. She looked faded, thought Connie, as if she wanted to dissolve away altogether. This must be Mrs Pope, Mrs Cartmell's companion.

'I am so sorry, Mrs Cartmell,' she said, twisting her fingers together.

'Where have you been, Muriel? You're very late!'

'I'm afraid I got lost.'

Mrs Cartmell rolled her eyes to heaven and Muriel Pope quaked.

'No problem, Mrs Pope,' said Louie Leblank cheerily. 'We have one life-preserver left. I thought we hadn't all our number here. I'll go fetch it myself before we give out the lifeboat stations.'

Elmer leaned across to Connie. 'Shall we go and explore? This will be boring.'

'Elmer!' thundered his mother, as Louie Leblank came up with Mrs Pope's life-preserver. 'You're to stay here, do you understand?'

'OK, Marmee.' Elmer subsided into his chair, sulky but subdued, his short-lived rebellion over. He cast a despairing look at Connie.

She sympathised, but she had promised Aunt Dorothea that she would look after Ida and Arthur, who, left to their own devices, would be completely hopeless and want to spend their entire time canoodling.

But at that very moment things stopped being boring altogether.

As the steward held up his hand for silence in order to announce the lifeboat stations, Muriel Pope rose to her feet in horror. Her terrible shriek echoed through the lounge.

Connie stared. The front of Mrs Pope's life-preserver was dripping down into her dowdy skirt. It was dark and sticky and looked horribly like blood.

3

Louie Leblank hurried back, gasping like a fish. 'My dear Mrs Pope!'

Arthur leaped to his feet. 'Oh, I say! Can I help? Mrs Pope, are you all right?'

'Clearly not!' said Mrs Cartmell. She looked affronted, as if this was yet another reason why she should never have employed Muriel Pope. 'Pass the woman my smelling salts, Elmer!' She plucked a small flask from her handbag.

Miss Pope, meanwhile, was feverishly ridding herself of the oozing life-preserver. She thrust it on the floor with a shudder, then sank back in her chair. She did not seem about to die, thought Connie, but definitely shocked all the same. Elmer, looking aghast, tried to offer her his mother's *sal volatile*, but it was waved away.

'May I call the ship's doctor?' said Louie Leblank.

'No – no, thank you. I am perfectly all right, not hurt at all.' Mrs Pope smiled weakly. 'I'm sorry to make such a silly fuss.'

Arthur picked up the life-preserver gingerly and examined it. 'Someone has inserted a phial of black oil into one of the pockets instead of the cork. It must have broken in half as you fastened it around you.'

'I think it might have caught on your brooch,' said Connie, but no one was listening.

'Just a prank,' said Louie Leblank. 'Must be one of the bellboys. I will have stern words. Leave it to me.'

He removed the life-preserver swiftly and gave orders for the black oil to be cleaned away. The saloon broke into subdued chatter. No one was quite sure what had happened, but all were curious to know. Rumours spread; a distinct atmosphere of unease filled the room.

The steward bustled about, bringing soothing cups of tea and slices of cake. Gradually the passengers calmed down, the lifeboat stations were given out and the room emptied as everyone went to change for dinner. Even Mrs Pope recovered after a cup of strong sweet tea.

'I think I might go and wash and change, if I may,'

she said meekly to Mrs Cartmell, who gave a dismissive nod.

Connie, Ida and Arthur were alone.

'Curious,' said Arthur. 'The oil was in one of those phials they use in the theatre. They usually have mock blood in them.'

'But who would want to play a trick on poor Mrs Pope?' said Ida.

'It just happened to be her,' Connie pointed out. 'Anyone might have come in late and been given the last life-preserver.'

'And if we don't watch it, *we'll* be late,' said Ida. 'For dinner. And I need at least an hour to change!'

Was there already a mystery on the *Princess May*? Connie was thoughtful as they went into the sumptious first-class dining saloon later.

Radmilla Oblomov had glass phials in her theatrical case. She seemed a most unlikely person to play a prank, but how would a bellboy have got hold of such a thing? Then there were the two actresses, Verina Vane and Dolores Devine, who might possibly be suspects too because of their theatrical connections.

Connie was seated with Ida and Arthur at Waldo Bamberger's table, with his other special guests, at the top of the long room. Full-length gilt mirrors, tinted a flattering peach to make even those most lacking in looks appear beautiful, reflected the vibrant silks and delicate chiffons of the ladies' gowns and the dazzlingly white evening dress of the gentlemen. The air was heavy with the scent of fresh hothouse lilies, masking any food smells, and the chandeliers overhead made the cut glass and silver cutlery glitter on the linen-covered tables.

Connie felt horribly buttoned up in her best muslin dress, and her sash, so beautifully tied by Ida, was squashed fatly and uncomfortably against her chair back. She was also extremely hungry; it seemed a long time since the cookies.

An exotic-looking pâté with tiny pieces of toast arrived first. It was so scrumptious that Connie finished hers before anyone else and looked around with interest at their table. She was always fascinated by people and noticed things most might not. And she wanted to keep a particular eye on Radmilla Oblomov, who was sitting on Mr Bamberger's left, dressed in a magnificent fringed crimson gown and feathered turban.

Mr Hiram Fink was looking grumpier than ever, and in his white tie as throttled as Connie felt. He probably hates being separated from his sheets of figures, she thought.

Mrs Cartmell was on Mr Bamberger's right, in pride of position and dignified in grey embroidered silk, a fox fur stole around her neck. Arthur sat next to Radmilla, looking flushed and shy. Ida, on the other side of the long table, kept a jealous eye on them both, but Arthur was too overcome to utter a word to his idol and busied himself with looking after Muriel Pope on his other side, asking politely after her recovery and passing her the salt for her soup.

Connie had Elmer next to her and on her other side a grey-faced, jowly man with bags under his eyes, who smelled strongly of cigarette smoke. His name was Biffer Smith, he told her abruptly – he was the journalist who was covering the voyage at Mr Bamberger's invitation. She thought she heard him mutter, 'He owes me a good story, that's why,' but perhaps she had misheard.

'My dear Mrs Pope,' said Mr Bamberger. 'Gee, I do apologise. I heard about what happened this afternoon. We shall find the joker, don't worry.'

'I am quite recovered, Mr Bamberger, I assure

you,' said Muriel Pope, blushing at being the centre of attention.

'That's the ticket, Mrs Pope. We'll replace your spoiled clothing at our expense. Plenty of good stores in New York. You know your Selfridges was started by a Yank?'

Muriel Pope nodded nervously. 'I've never visited but I'm sure it's very nice.'

'Oh, it is!' cried Ida, who, after one summer as an heiress, was already an authority on London shops.

Around the table little bubbles of conversation broke out. Connie listened and tucked in; she had never had such wonderful food.

In between courses poor Arthur had to leap up and play the most popular tunes of the moment. People talked over his playing in the rudest way. 'Not good for the old digestion,' he said with a laugh to Muriel Pope, when he came to sit down again, rather flushed and hot after playing a complicated ragtime piece.

'Mr George Cohan said he would audition me personally for his new musical,' said one of the actresses to the other.

'Broadway, here we come!' said her friend, with a giggle.

They were very pretty: one dark, one fair. Both had

pouting crimson lips, matching nail varnish and thin arched eyebrows. They wore the latest tunics and underskirts in pale blue and lemon yellow chiffon respectively, with matching bandeaux. Connie watched them carefully while she listened to the conversation around her.

'Diaghilev – he's so frightened of water,' Radmilla was saying to Mr Bamberger. 'When he said he wanted to send me to see zis man instead of him, what could I say? I had to do it for him. But it is – how you say – hush, hush? He doesn't want it in the newspapers.' She eyed Biffer Smith.

'It's OK, honey,' said Mr Bamberger. Connie was interested to see him place his hand over hers. 'Biffer is under strict instructions.'

Connie looked at Biffer Smith's powerful fingers, which were clenched around his fork. They looked as if they would snap its silver stem in two, let alone a pen.

'Have you been a boxer?' she enquired politely, by way of conversation.

He had been gazing at Radmilla with something like admiration in his baggy eyes, but at Connie's question, they swivelled to her, startled. 'A boxer? Hell, no. Why do you ask?'

'You look like one, that's all,' said Connie, before she realised it might be rather rude.

He stared at her. 'You go to a lot of fights, do you?'

'Well, no,' she admitted. 'It would be most interesting, but I don't think my aunts would like it if I did.' She frowned. 'Why are you called Biffer then?'

'It's usually me who asks the questions,' said Biffer Smith. 'If you really want to know, young lady, it's because my stories biff 'em hard between the eyes. I've got a reputation for telling the truth and it hits home. My readers respect that.'

Connie wanted to tell him that she, too, liked discovering the truth – in a scientific manner, of course – but with the arrival of the fish course, he had turned away with some alacrity to Ida on his other side.

Hiram Fink glared across at her. 'In my day, children weren't allowed to stay up to dinner, Waldo,' he said pointedly. 'Certainly not to converse.'

'I have to stay up to dinner,' Connie explained calmly. 'You see, I'm Miss Fairbanks's chaperone.' She ignored Mr Fink's splutter and the giggles from the two actresses.

'Scandalous!' muttered Mrs Cartmell, though everyone heard her. 'I wouldn't allow them to set foot in my hotels!'

'Connie is a very special child, Hiram,' said Mr Bamberger equally loudly, to Mr Fink. 'And Elmer, too,' he added, as Mrs Cartmell began to bristle.

'Of course, I never think of Elmer as a child,' she said. 'He's my little assistant, aren't you, dear? Always at my side.'

Elmer bit his lip and stared at his plate.

At last everyone finished their poached salmon. It really was astonishing how long grown-ups took to eat their food. There was laughter at the top of the table where Mr Bamberger was enjoying his wine and growing more genial with every sip. Even Radmilla's stern, sculptured features relaxed. Nothing he said, however, could make Mrs Cartmell smile. There was something bitter about her downturned mouth, Connie thought.

Her son Elmer sat meekly and silently beside Connie, his hair swept into its immaculate quiff, his clothes a miniature version of an adult's white tie and tails. Now and then Connie noticed that he blinked anxiously at his mother.

Biffer Smith was now deep in conversation with Ida. Ida opened her beautiful blue eyes very wide at him and played with her food. Connie hoped she was being discreet and not telling him anything about inheriting the Fairbanks fortune. They had had enough trouble with journalists already.

She sighed to herself as she ate her Chicken à la Maryland. It was altogether rather too much responsibility now she had both Ida and Arthur to look after.

Ida was agog. 'But how perfectly dreadful, Mr Smith!' Then 'Not really?' and 'Oh, what a tragic story!'

Mr Bamberger must have keen hearing. 'Biffer!' he called out jovially. 'And what story might that be?'

'I was telling Miss Fairbanks about the death of that poor young mechanic, Waldo,' said Biffer Smith. 'If you remember, I didn't write about it at your request.'

Mr Bamberger's soft, smiling features stiffened. 'It was good of you, Biffer.'

One of the actresses leaned across, fluttering her long eyelashes. 'Oh, do tell, Mr Bamberger. It sounds most mysterious. What happened exactly?'

The table quietened. Everyone looked up from their chicken. Perhaps they had heard 'tragic accident' or perhaps they were bored talking to their neighbour, but around them the people at the other tables seemed to hush, too.

Mr Bamberger sighed, as if it was a story he had told too often.

'As you all know, the *Princess May* was built in Southampton. She had left the slipway and was afloat for the completion of work to her superstructure. The young guy in question was on a platform hanging from a gantry, fixing one of the last bolts on the side of the ship. He must have lost his balance. Maybe gotten dizzy or some such. He fell. Couldn't swim, it turned out after. The men tried to find him—'

Biffer Smith interrupted. 'All they could find were his yellow overalls, floating on the surface of the water in a patch of oil. That's right, isn't it, Waldo? They never found his body.'

Mr Bamberger nodded sombrely. 'Tragic accidents sometimes happen during the building of a ship.'

'He was only fifteen,' said Biffer Smith. 'His first job.'

'I didn't know anything about that,' said Mr Bamberger. 'My foreman employed the technicians, of course. They were all keen to work on an enterprise like this.'

'So it's not true that the gantry was faulty?'

Waldo Bamberger's normally affable face flushed a

deep red but he spoke quietly. 'I'll thank you not to spread rumours, Biffer. That's bunk and you know it.'

Connie looked at Biffer Smith. His mouth was compressed and his grey boxer's face pugnacious. It was altogether rather impolite of him to bring it up in the first place, she thought, when he was on board at Mr Bamberger's expense. She wondered why he had done it.

The mood of gaiety had suddenly gone. Radmilla Oblomov flipped her fringes out of the way and frowned sternly into her wine. Hiram Fink stared at Biffer Smith, his face angry; the two actresses looked at each other, wide-eyed. Cornelia Cartmell pursed her lips.

'That poor young lad,' sighed Ida.

Muriel Pope had tears in her eyes: she seemed altogether overcome, her fork clattering on to her plate as she faltered, 'I do hope his death won't bring the ship bad luck, Mr Bamberger!'

4

No scientist worthy of the name believed in superstition, Connie knew, so neither would she. And after a surprised silence round the table, no one else appeared to take Muriel Pope's comment too seriously either.

The guests recovered their spirits and Mr Bamberger himself, his good humour restored, escorted Ida to the ballroom, where Arthur continued to play with great aplomb. Connie left Ida dancing with all the gentlemen who had been at their table and several more; it was remarkable the way that Ida was always so popular.

She went down the deserted passage to her stateroom. Something on the floor caught the overhead light as she passed. She turned and saw it was a small black spot, oily and glistening and not much bigger than a penny coin. She bent down to have a closer look.

'Hi, Miss Constance!' a voice hissed. 'What are you doing?'

'Why are you creeping behind me, Elmer?'

'I thought we could do a spot of detective work together, like your Mr Sherlock Holmes always does. You know, work out who had played that prank with the life-preserver.'

'Sherlock Holmes isn't a real person,' Connie pointed out. He looked so crushed she decided to be generous. 'But I have found this.' She pointed to the floor.

'Wow!' said Elmer. 'It's a clue, isn't it? It must have been left by the culprit!'

Connie sighed to herself. She began to search along the passage.

'What are you doing now, Miss Constance?'

'Seeing if there are any more spots. There might be a whole trail of them.' Connie relented. 'You can help me if you like.'

Elmer's eyes shone. 'Lolla palooza! Sure thing, Miss Constance!'

They both looked, but there were no more to be seen.

Connie pulled out a handkerchief. 'I'm going to take a sample.'

'What are you going to do with it, Miss Constance?'

'I don't know yet,' said Connie, 'but it might be useful. It's what scientists should do.' She bent down and poked a corner of the thin linen into the oil spot. It had the unfortunate result of spreading it further, so that there was now a noticeable smear near one of the stateroom doors. It was, she realised, Radmilla Oblomov's stateroom: number 55.

'Hi there, kiddos,' said Louie Leblank, appearing suddenly behind them. He patted Elmer on the head. 'Good to see you again, young man.' Elmer frowned and ducked away, but it didn't stop Leblank from asking Connie, 'And what are we up to here?'

'If you really want to know,' said Elmer grandly, 'we were—'

He stopped as Connie trod heavily on his shoe. She screwed the hanky into a ball in the palm of her hand. Louie Leblank's face was as smooth and smiling as ever; she wasn't sure whether he had seen her bend down or not.

'Just chatting, Mr Leblank,' she said.

'Good that you're becoming pals. ''Fraid you're a bit outnumbered on this trip!' His face altered. He frowned down. 'That's a nasty mess. Whatever is it? I must get one of the bellboys to clean it up.'

He hurried off.

'You nearly gave us away!' Connie said crossly to Elmer. 'Detectives always keep their methods quiet until they've found the culprit. We don't know yet whether Mr Leblank didn't do it. He gave the life-preserver to Mrs Pope after all.'

'Sorry, Miss Constance,' said Elmer meekly.

'And for goodness sake, call me Connie!'

'Detectives', indeed! Why had she let Elmer think he was her accomplice, just as if it were a game?

Back in the stateroom, a steward had drawn the curtains to shut out the dark sea outside the window and made both beds ready for the night. Connie's had been pulled down from the wall and a corner of the bedclothes turned back at the top.

Picking up the enticing new notebook and a pencil from the desk, she climbed on to Ida's bed, which looked even more comfortable than her own, and settled back against the pillows. She opened the notebook at the first crisp white page. She thought she would make a list of the people she had met so far, like a proper anthropologist should do.

After that she wrote a heading:

Mrs Pope's oily life-preserver
Possible suspects:

Radmilla Oblomov – owns vanity case full of
grease paints, etc.
Dolores Devine – must have access to theatre stuff,
could have brought on board
Verina Vane, actress – ditto
Louie Leblank – gave life-preserver to Mrs P (after
tampering with?)
A bellboy's prank?
Motive ???

The engines made a soft thrum in Connie's ears and every now and then the boat shifted gently beneath her, like an animal stirring in its slumber. It was curiously soothing. Her eyelids closed and the pencil fell from her hand.

She was woken by Ida entering the cabin in a headlong rush. Connie blinked up at her. Even half asleep she could see that Ida's face was very white in the bedside light. Her voice when she spoke was high.

'Connie! Wake up! I've just seen a ghost!'

Ida put her hands to her face. 'I saw it in the distance, disappearing down the passage outside!'

Connie had never seen a ghost. As a budding scientist, of course, she didn't believe in them, but all the same she was curious. She came awake instantly, scrambled off the bed and sprang to the door. Opening it quietly, she stuck her head out and peered down the passage.

The lights had been dimmed: it must be the middle of the night at least, and the passage was silent and distinctly eerie. The stateroom doors were all shut, the passengers inside presumably asleep.

To her great disappointment there was no sign of any ghost.

She was about to close the door when something happened at the far end of the passage. For a single terrifying moment a figure appeared at the bend, an apparition in yellow. Then as quickly it disappeared, as if it had simply faded away.

The hairs rose on Connie's scalp. Her heart seemed to stop. But a rational mind like hers should not believe in ghosts. After a few stunned seconds she didn't hesitate. She closed the door behind her and began to run towards the bend where the ghost had disappeared.

She reached it, out of breath. Very cautiously, she looked down the parallel passage. There was absolutely nothing to be seen, except another row of closed doors, the rooms for the stewards and bellboys. She waited but the passage remained empty until two stewards appeared, very much alive and talking in low voices to one another.

'Can I help you, miss?' one of them asked, looking curiously at Connie's slept-in dress and her trailing sash.

She shook her head and retreated.

Back in their stateroom Ida was sitting stiffly on the edge of her bed.

Connie put an arm round her. 'There's nothing out there, Ida. What exactly did you see?'

'It was the overalls! I saw this figure at the end of our passage, dressed in yellow overalls. It was the ghost of that young engineer, Connie – the one who drowned while this ship was being built!'

Ida gulped and steadied herself. 'I left Arthur playing in the ballroom – about midnight, it was – and took the lift to our deck on my own. I had to work out which side our room was from the diagram on

44

the notice – port or starboard – it's so muddling! – then when I did, there was this ghastly spectre at the far end of our passage. When I looked round, it had gone!'

'It wasn't a ghost, only a workman,' said Connie soothingly.

Ida fanned herself with a dinner menu from her evening bag and shook her head. 'You know me, Connie. It's not like me to be so blooming fanciful. But I tell you, ghost or not, I think Mrs Pope is right. This ship is doomed!'

5

The next morning Connie was woken by the sun streaming through the crack in the curtains. Ida's little clock said eight fifteen. Ida herself was snoring gently, smiling in her sleep as if she were dreaming of Arthur and hadn't another care in the world, the spectral figure from last night quite forgotten.

Connie flung on her clothes, frowning over her buttons and the sash on her pinafore. She crammed her boater over her hair, which she didn't bother to brush – its tangles looked a bit like ringlets anyway, she decided. Then in her new soft-soled deck shoes she made her way to the Promenade deck. She wasn't going to waste a moment of her first day at sea.

The deck was almost deserted, apart from two male passengers in the distance playing quoits. It seemed to involve throwing rope circles into numbered squares and a good deal of cursing as the quoits were blown sideways by the wind, which was fresher today.

Connie held on to her boater, clasped the sun-warmed wooden rail with her other hand and gazed out. Brilliant spears of sunlight sparkled on the surface of the ocean. She could feel warmth on her back and taste salt on her tongue. The great ship was gliding steadily through the waves, with a little roll now and then, so that she had to plant her feet apart.

'Miss Carew! Up bright and early!'

'And so are you, Mr Leblank.'

'It's my job, Miss Carew. Checking things, you know.'

Connie looked at Mr Bamberger's entertainment manager with grudging respect; she approved of checking things.

Louie Leblank, dazzling today in a striped blazer, put a hand on Connie's back. 'Let me show you the area Mr Bamberger has reserved for his guests. Come with me, little lady, out of the wind.'

He led Connie to the other side of the ship. It was much less windy here and there was a roped area where long wooden deckchairs, with labels hanging over their backs, had been placed in a row in the sun.

'Sometimes the decks get very crowded later in the day if the weather is good, and all the deckchairs get

47

taken.' Louie Leblank clasped his hands together. 'And I see someone is already making use of hers!'

It was Muriel Pope, who got to her feet in a fluster, dislodging her mending. 'Oh dear, Mr Leblank! I hope it wasn't very wrong of me! I am on the right one, I think!' Her voice trailed away helplessly, while Connie ran to retrieve a cotton reel that had rolled across the deck, leaving a line of thread behind it.

'Don't concern yourself, Mrs Pope. I'll leave you two to get to know each other. You'll remember Miss Carew?'

Connie wound the thread back round the reel, as she had had to do so many times for Aunt Dorothea. 'Would you like me to put it in there?' She pointed to the large tapestry reticule sitting beside Mrs Pope's chair.

'It's very kind of you, dear –' Mrs Pope took it from her '– but I need some more thread for my needle.'

Connie looked down at the crêpe-de-chine spread out on Mrs Pope's lap. 'What are you making?'

'I'm only sewing a button back on one of Mrs Cartmell's blouses.' Mrs Pope sighed. 'One of my little jobs is to look after her clothes and hats.'

Connie thought that Cornelia Cartmell probably had rather a lot of both those. She sat down awkwardly;

she didn't feel she could leave now without looking rude.

'I'd be careful sitting in these chairs, if I were you,' Muriel Pope said. 'They don't look very strong.' She sighed again. 'Oh, dear, my eyesight's not what it was!' She was peering through spectacles at the needle she was trying to thread.

'Let me do it for you,' said Connie, and did so. She noticed that Mrs Pope was wearing her brooch again, at the neck of her blouse. Its ornate fretwork glinted dully in the sun. 'Such a pretty brooch,' she said kindly.

Muriel Pope patted it and gave a small smile. 'My husband gave it to me when we first met.' Her mouth twisted out of its smile. 'Then two years later he ran off and left me! Beware of men, my dear.'

'I suppose Mrs Cartmell is still asleep,' said Connie, after a difficult silence. 'Have you been with her long?'

Mrs Pope gave a short breathless laugh. 'Only a couple of weeks or so. I'm fortunate, I suppose. I think if she'd had longer to look, she never would have offered me the position. It's only for the voyage, you see. She's made that quite clear.'

Connie wasn't surprised; it was obvious to everyone that Mrs Cartmell had already decided her companion was useless.

'I must go to her in a minute and check that her breakfast has arrived.' Mrs Pope laid down her mending. 'But it's so nice and peaceful here. I didn't sleep well. All night long I kept hearing feet tramping up and down outside.'

Connie pricked up her ears. 'In the passage outside your stateroom?'

'No, no, it was on the deck. Tramp, tramp, tramp all night. As if someone was wearing heavy sea boots.'

'Did you look out?'

'I couldn't bring myself to do it.' Muriel Pope gave a little shudder. 'I was too frightened. Silly, I know. I thought it might be . . .' She folded the blouse and slipped the delicate material carefully into her tapestry bag. She rose to her feet, her long skirt limp around her ankles. 'But I don't want to upset you. You're only a child. I shouldn't be telling you this.'

Connie had often found that if she didn't say much and listened, grown-ups would forget her age and tell her interesting things. And she was interested in what Mrs Cartmell's companion had said. Did Muriel Pope believe she had heard the ghostly footsteps of the drowned boy?

But unfortunately Mrs Pope was already hurrying off, her stoop more pronounced as she clutched her reticule against her chest.

It was time for breakfast, time to go and wake Ida. Connie was about to jump up when a voice said, 'Ah, ze little girl who brought me my make-up case!'

It was Radmilla Oblomov, formidable in a masculine shirt and tie and ankle-length pleated skirt.

'Hello, Miss Oblomov,' said Connie. She had thought famous people stayed in bed for most of the morning.

'Madame, please. I have a husband somewhere, I zink. But you, little one, may call me Radmilla.'

Connie was doubtful she would ever be able to call so grand a creature by her first name, but she was aware of the honour. 'Have you had breakfast already?'

Radmilla pouted. 'Ah, ze breakfast! No caviare! No smoked salmon! Vhat I put up with to do what Sergei wants! A gymnasium without ze barre, so I must practise in ze – how do you say? – toilette – with ze towel rail!'

'You could practise in the ballroom,' said Connie. 'There won't be anyone there during the day.' Except for Arthur rehearsing his music and how pleased he would be to find his heroine there!

'Vhat a quite excellent idea, my dear! Sergei will be

pleased to hear I keep up my movements even on ze sea.'

'Who is Sergei?'

Radmilla looked at Connie in bemusement. 'Why, ze great Diaghilev, of course. Impresario, director of ze famous Ballets Russes, ze toast of Paris and ze whole of Europe! And soon to come to New York, if I can persuade zem. Diaghilev has given me zis great responsibility and zo I must take it. He hates the water, you understand, zo I have to come instead.'

Connie looked suitably impressed. She wondered how good the Americans would be at deciphering Radmilla's somewhat thick Russian accent.

Radmilla prowled behind her, swishing her pleats about. 'Vhere iz my name on all zis cardboard? I cannot read zese. I wish to zit down. I have been up since dawn doing pliés in ze toilette.'

'How very tiring,' said Connie. She scrambled off her deckchair. 'I'll have a look but I'm sure it doesn't matter which one you sit on.'

'Oh, but it does,' said Radmilla. 'In Russia we have rules for ze highest and ze low and zey must be kept. Ballerinas, zey are −' she raised the palms of her hands in a dramatic gesture '− celebrated in

Moscow. It iz a city of ze highest culture. So I expect a most special deckchair.'

'I think they're all the same,' said Connie.

She found Radmilla's chair and pointed it out to her. It was, in fact, placed a little way away from the others and had cushions with blue and white stripes. Mrs Cartmell would be put out.

Radmilla swept over. 'Zank you,' she said graciously and was about to sit down when Connie noticed something.

'Wait a moment, madame.'

The slat that the back of the deckchair slotted into looked broken. If Radmilla Oblomov had sat down or lain back in it, it would have collapsed.

'Vat is ze matter?' said the dancer impatiently.

Connie pointed. 'It's not safe.'

'Vat?' Radmilla peered closer. 'Vhy, you are right!' She stared at Connie, her dark eyes large and dramatic. 'Someone vishes me to dance no longer! Is zat it? Sergei said I must take care not to have no accident. You, my child, have saved me from ze broken back! Zank you, zank you!'

The next moment Radmilla's arms went round Connie in a tight hug and Connie was pressed against her bony bosom. She gasped for air. Radmilla smelled of an intoxicating musky scent and, rather more strongly, of sweat.

Connie rescued her boater as she was released and crammed it back on. 'I'm sure it's not deliberate,' she said soothingly. 'Whoever put the deckchairs out this morning didn't notice this one was damaged. I'll tell a steward.'

'*Nyet*, you are wrong!' wailed Radmilla. 'Zere is someone on zis ship zat vishes me never to dance again! I have zo many rivals in the ballet, jealous of me!'

Connie was a little while fetching another deckchair. She swapped the cushions over and Radmilla allowed herself to be persuaded to sit down, though she then sat bolt upright, glowering at the sunlit sea. 'I should not have come,' Connie heard her mutter. 'Zat man! He makes everyone do his vishes!' No doubt she was talking about Sergei again. He sounded as bad as Mrs Cartmell.

'I should go to breakfast now, if you are all right,' said Connie. Her stomach was rumbling and she thought Ida's must be too.

Radmilla looked at her tragically. 'I am not all right. I have an enemy on board who vants to hurt me! Breakfast, pah! But go, child, go! You know nothing of Diaghilev, or of dancing!'

As Connie went down to her stateroom to see if Ida was awake, she puzzled over the incident. She had had a good look at the damaged deckchair when she swapped it over. She couldn't be sure, but it looked as if someone had tried to saw through the back slat. Had it been done to injure Radmilla Oblomov deliberately, to stop her dancing, as she said? It must have been done after Louie Leblank had done his checking, unless he had done it himself. And it meant that Radmilla was probably no longer a suspect as far as the oily life-preserver was concerned.

The other decidedly odd thing was that it looked as if the same black oil had been dropped deliberately on to the slat. She had quickly taken a sample of it with her hanky so that she could compare it with the one from yesterday evening.

At this rate she'd soon be running out of clean handkerchiefs.

6

Mr Bamberger's long table in the first-class dining saloon was only half full for breakfast. Connie was disappointed to find that Mr Bamberger wasn't there, but he had said he would take many of his meals with the captain.

Biffer Smith sat somewhere in the middle of the table, Muriel Pope facing him and venturing a polite remark every now and then, which was largely ignored. Connie, Ida and Arthur sat at one end; Hiram Fink, buried in an extremely dull-looking tome, as far away as possible at the other. When Radmilla Oblomov glided in a little later demanding coffee he didn't even look up, though Biffer Smith goggled at her shirt and tie.

'I say,' said Arthur, as he wolfed down his kidneys and bacon, 'a decent breakfast is just what a chap needs after a long night!'

'Will you have to work so hard tonight, dearest?' asked Ida tenderly. She was wearing the first of her cruise costumes – a striking divided skirt striped in blue and white, with a sailor top in the same blue. It matched her eyes to perfection.

''Fraid so. It's in my contract, you see.'

Ida looked crestfallen. 'But couldn't we have just one dance together? I was so lonely yesterday evening.'

'As far as I remember you had a whole queue of gents wanting to dance with you,' said Arthur, but he laid his hand on hers. 'We can spend most of the day together, sweetheart, though I should do a little practising sometime.'

Connie smiled to herself. How pleased he would be to find Radmilla Oblomov in the ballroom executing her pliés!

'And Connie must come with us, of course,' said Arthur. 'Since she's our chaperone.'

'Of course,' echoed Ida, but she didn't sound quite so enthusiastic.

'I can stay at a discreet distance,' Connie muttered. 'That's what chaperones do, isn't it?'

Ida leaped up and planted a warm kiss on her cheek. 'Oh, Connie, you're such a dear! And you rescued me last night from the ghost!'

'I didn't really,' murmured Connie, mollified. 'I don't think there was one . . .' but her words weren't heard.

'Ghost?' said Biffer Smith. He craned across. Connie thought she could even see his nose twitching, as if he scented a story.

'Ghost!' exclaimed Muriel Pope. 'Why I saw one too − or rather heard one! All night, tramping about on the deck outside.'

There was a flurry of excited conversation, in which Hiram Fink took no part but sighed deeply. Biffer Smith pulled a green-backed notebook from his breast pocket and began to write. Connie could imagine the headline:

Shipboard Spectres! Passengers' Peril on *Princess May*!

Poor Mr Bamberger!

And then, to make matters worse, Radmilla Oblomov stood up, with a furious twirl of her pleats. The entire dining saloon stilled and gazed at her as if spellbound, especially Biffer Smith.

'Vhy, someone zis very morning has tried to cripple me for life, to stop me dancing! Me, greatest ballerina of the Ballets Russes, might have suffered with a broken back if it vasn't for my little friend here!' She gestured at Connie and stared around defiantly. 'So who did zis terrible zing? Who?'

The dining saloon stared back but was silent.

Biffer Smith scribbled on.

A nasty prank, a spectral figure, ghostly footsteps and now a deliberate attempt to injure one of Mr Bamberger's guests. Biffer Smith was certainly getting the story he wanted, thought Connie, as she led the way up to the promenade deck, Ida and Arthur behind her.

When they passed the Purser's notice-board there was a chart, showing the route they would be taking to America and the Island of Manhattan through mysterious loops and circles. Arthur explained they showed the different depths of the Atlantic Ocean.

An arrow pointed to the location of the *Princess May* at 1200 midnight the previous night. It looked as if she had a very long way to go and Connie wasn't sure the ship could win the Blue Riband for the fastest passage to New York, even with her revolutionary new turbine engines.

A sheet of paper was pinned up, listing events taking place during the voyage – quizzes, deck quoits and slider competitions – signed Louie Leblank, Entertainment Manager.

'How jolly,' cried Ida. 'There's going to be a fancy dress party for first-class passengers on the last night!'

'Will I have to dress up?' Arthur said doubtfully.

'Of course! It says we can hire costumes from the purser's office.'

Arthur looked gloomy.

'There's going to be a solo by Radmilla Oblomov,' said Connie. '*The Dying Swan*.' She grinned. 'Good thing I rescued her before her back was broken and she did actually die! And look, Arthur, you're to accompany her!'

'I hope she has the music,' he said. 'We shall have to rehearse. I've only played Saint-Saëns's piece once.' But he seemed considerably cheered.

The sun was still sparkling on the sea when they reached the promenade deck. Connie showed them the roped-off area that Mr Bamberger had reserved for his guests. Mrs Pope's deckchair was empty and Radmilla Oblomov had not risked a return.

Mrs Cartmell was lying full length, her eyes half

closed under an enormous, chiffon-veiled hat. Elmer was mooching about, walking the length of the deckchairs and back again. 'I do wish you'd sit down!' his mother snapped from beneath her brim.

Elmer caught sight of Connie and brightened. 'Hello, Miss Connie!'

Mrs Cartmell sat up abruptly. 'Come along, Elmer. I think the wind is becoming a little cold.'

'But Marmee . . .' Elmer cast a despairing look at Connie as he disappeared in his mother's wake.

'That woman cut me!' said Ida. 'She cut you, too, Arthur! She definitely doesn't want to know us. She thinks we're improper because we've got darling Connie as our chaperone.'

'How ridiculous,' said Arthur staunchly.

Connie couldn't have cared less. She didn't give two hoots for Mrs Cartmell and Elmer was drippy not to stand up to her.

They looked around at the row of empty deckchairs. It appeared that some of Mr Bamberger's guests had enjoyed the sun for a while and then left. There were empty glasses by the actresses' chairs and an ashtray with two stubbed-out cigarettes by Biffer Smith's. Mr Fink's chair had been pushed out of line as if he, too, had sat there at some point.

Arthur had a book of sheet music, which he settled down to study. Connie was in the middle of *The Nicest Girl in the School* by Angela Brazil, but she was distracted by Ida, who was gripping the wooden rail and peering down at the water.

'There's so much blooming sea, isn't there?' she said, a little dolefully. 'It just goes on and on for ever, moving about all the time and never stopping.'

'Until it reaches land,' said Connie.

'But land's a long way off, isn't it? Four more days! And meanwhile, there's nothing to see but water!'

Of course it was the first time Ida had seen the sea, thought Connie. The vastness of the Atlantic Ocean must be rather a shock. She considered herself a seasoned sailor, having once travelled on the ferry to the Isle of Wight with her parents when she was eight.

Ida jumped up and began moving her deckchair around.

'Whatever are you doing, dearest?' asked Arthur.

'I can't bear to look at it any longer. It's just too big.'

For a short while all was peaceful. The thrum of the engines was gentle, the sea rushed by below the side of the ship and a soft breeze turned the pages of Connie's book for her. Ida sat with her back to the sea, contentedly facing a ventilator shaft and flipping through the new issue of *Home Chips*.

'My sunhat!' she wailed suddenly. 'I should be wearing my hat! My face will go all brown and wrinkly.'

'Shall I get it?' said Arthur, looking up from his music book.

'You won't know where to find it. We could go together and get it. Connie, you won't mind being left, will you? We won't be long at all.'

Ida took Arthur firmly by the arm and waltzed him off, past the bellboy opening the inside door for them. The next moment they were gone.

Connie took out the two stained hankies from her pocket and examined them. Yes, it was definitely the same oil. Dark and glutinous and with a rather nasty smell, even though it was dry now. So that probably meant the same hand had spilled it on both occasions – in the passage and on Radmilla's deckchair. It was a pity she hadn't taken a sample from the life-preserver, but she was almost sure it would have matched the others.

She rolled the hankies up together and stuffed them back into her pinafore pocket.

Ida and Arthur seemed to be being a long time. She forgot about them, though, as she read on, until a creaking made her realise that someone had sat down next to her and was now giving a polite cough, as if wanting to be noticed.

'Hello again, Miss Connie,' said Elmer.

'I thought you'd gone off with your mother,' said Connie. Sighing, she put down her book.

'I escaped!' he said, with small triumphant smile. 'She doesn't need me at the moment. She's inspecting the ladies' health salon, in case she wants to put one into her hotels.'

'She shouldn't copy Mr Bamberger's ideas,' Connie said.

Elmer shrugged. 'You don't know my mother.'

'I know she's being very rude to Ida.'

'She's told me not to talk to the three of you but I shan't take any notice.' Elmer leaned closer. 'Say, have you found any more clues?' He looked as if he was bursting to tell her something.

'Clues?'

'To the joker. I heard about Miss Oblomov's deckchair. They're saying that it was covered in oil, too, like the life-preserver.'

'Who said that?' said Connie, startled. 'I didn't tell anyone. I don't think Radmilla Oblomov even realised.'

Elmer looked vague. 'Oh, I don't know. My mother

says gossip spreads like wildfire. She never wants a scandal in her hotels in case it gets into the newspapers and people stop coming.'

Connie frowned. 'But it would be a disaster for Mr Bamberger if people didn't want to travel on the *Princess May*!'

The steward who removed the deckchair must have said something, she thought. Who else could have known about the oil? Except whoever damaged it, of course.

'I think Biffer Smith has already written about it,' said Elmer. 'He's keeping a journal of the voyage.'

'Then I must tell him it isn't true!' cried Connie.

'Is it?'

'Well, yes,' Connie admitted. 'But there was only a tiny bit of oil. I don't think it was a prank, though. It was actually rather dangerous.'

His eyes widened. 'So you mean next time it could be worse?'

She shrugged. 'There probably won't be a next time.'

'But we ought to find out who did it. I think,' Elmer added, with bashful pride, 'that I may have found a clue.'

Connie frowned. 'What do you mean?'

7

The paper was yellowed and creased and as light as
air, though Connie could feel that there was something
in the fold. She opened it carefully before it was blown
out of her hands.

It held a curl of dark hair. She wrapped it up
again quickly.

'Where did you find this?'

'It was caught under the slat of my deckchair.
I noticed it when I sat down. I think the wind blew it
there. Someone must have dropped it. It could belong
to whoever sawed through Miss Oblomov's chair!'

'But again, it might not,' said Connie.

'Are you going to keep it? As another sample?'

Connie shook her head. 'We ought to put it back
under the slat in case someone misses it. I'm afraid it's
not a clue, Elmer. People do keep locks of hair. My
cousin Ida had a locket with her mother's hair in it.'

'My marm had one too, with my baby hair,' said Elmer, but he looked a little cast down. Connie glanced at his hair, which had escaped out of its sleeked quiff in the wind. It was brown and curly in its natural state – quite nice hair, in fact.

She opened her book again, but it was hopeless trying to read with Elmer asking questions and mentioning his mother every second sentence. She took pity on him at last.

'Do you want to go and explore? Now your mother's out of the way, I mean?'

He leaped up as if he had been waiting for the invitation. 'Lolla palooza! Swell idea, Miss Connie! Only we'd better not go near the ladies' health salon!'

'No jolly fear!' said Connie.

But it was already too late. From the other double doors at the far end of the deck a voice boomed, 'Elmer! Whatever are you doing? I expressly forbade you to—'

'Quick!' said Connie, as Mrs Cartmell launched herself out on deck and immediately lost her hat in the wind. While his mother was distracted, Connie grabbed Elmer and dragged him to the nearest exit. With a conspiratorial grin the bellboy opened the door and they ran through.

The lift was already waiting at their level. Connie closed the outer door with a clash and the last thing they saw was the outraged face of Mrs Cartmell as she strode down the deck as fast as her long skirts and the wind would allow her.

As the lift descended, Elmer's voice was a squeak of terrror. 'But my marm—'

'You can say I kidnapped you,' said Connie. 'Do you always do what your mother wants?'

'Yes,' said Elmer simply.

Connie hadn't realised quite how many passengers there were on the ship. The second and steerage classes had their own dining saloons and were not allowed into the first-class rooms because they had bought cheaper tickets – which perhaps was fair. But the second-class dining saloon seemed almost as grand as the first-class one.

Elmer informed Connie knowledgeably that steerage would be crammed with Irish immigrants: they were travelling to America to find jobs. His father had told him about the immigrants on his own transatlantic ships.

They explored several lounges, full of potted palms, overstuffed chairs and polished mahogany tables. Elmer trailed after Connie, looking thrilled and terrified by her daring as she poked her nose into the steamy Turkish baths; they caught a glimpse of several enormous naked men wallowing before they were driven out by a furious attendant. They avoided the stuffy Gentlemen's Smoking Room but found the Gymnasium. It looked fun, with its exercise bicycle, climbing bars and a bucking legless horse you could ride on, but as soon as they went to investigate a steward shooed them out again.

The Reading and Writing Room was completely silent except for the scratching of pens and the turning of pages, so they tiptoed through and found themselves in a long gallery where people were playing cards on baize-covered tables, murmuring to each other, and every now and then slapping their cards down and shouting something out, such as 'You jammy blighter!' or 'I call that a pretty poor show, Ponsonby!'

The women seemed just as competitive as the men, crying, 'Oh, Johnnie,' or 'Charlie, you duffer!' at their partners.

At this lower level the waves looked much bigger through the portholes.

'Let's sit down,' said Elmer. He looked a little green.

A steward popped up as soon as they sat down. Connie ordered two lemonades and a plate of cream buns and signed her name and stateroom number with a grand flourish on the bill.

Elmer, it seemed, had been impressed by their tour of the ship which, he reluctantly admitted, rivalled his father's finest.

Connie was glad she had Elmer alone. She leaned across to him and said in a whisper, 'What do you know about Louie Leblank?'

Elmer scowled at once.

'He's a louse. He spread stories about Marmee and Pop to the press when they split. Pop didn't know but I think my mother suspected. My father had been good to him, too, giving him a job when he was only a washed-up mimic.'

'You mean he'd been in the theatre?' said Connie eagerly.

Elmer nodded. 'He'd been doing shipboard entertainment.' His face brightened. 'Why? You think he really could be a suspect? Lolla palooza! But what's his motive?'

Connie smiled mysteriously and said nothing more. Louie Leblank might be working secretly for

Mr Cartmell, trying to ruin the reputation of a rival ship. He would have been able to damage Radmilla's deckchair first thing that morning without anyone seeing. He would also have been able to interfere with Mrs Pope's life-preserver.

She couldn't tell Elmer, of course: he'd defend any slur on his father. Besides – remembering her list of suspects – there were other people who might have secret motives, too. In fact, it might be any one of Mr Bamberger's guests with a personal grudge against him.

After he had eaten several cream buns Elmer became very quiet. He gazed at the waves, mesmerised. Down as low in the ship as this, the motion was more pronounced and Connie could feel the vibration of the turbine engines through the table.

After a while he scrambled to his feet, looking greener than ever.

'Goodbye, Miss Connie. I should get back to Marmee. She'll be worried.'

And he almost ran from the gallery, his hand to his mouth.

Outside Mrs Cartmell's stateroom a bellboy was scrubbing away at the floor with a cloth. He looked up with a wide apologetic grin on his freckled face as Connie tried to step past him. He wore his red pill-box hat at a rakish angle on his sandy hair and was fast growing out of his jacket and black trousers. When he stood up, he was tall and gawky and slightly knock-kneed.

'Won't be a mo, miss. Don't get this on your shoes. Gotta get it cleaned up for Her Majesty.' He flicked his thumb at Mrs Cartmell's door. 'She rang her bell for me in a right rage. Said she'd got it on the hem of her skirt.'

'What is it?' asked Connie, but she knew.

'Oil, miss, but where it came from, only the Almighty knows. She said she might have slipped in it and broke her leg. Drips right outside her stateroom for all the world to see.'

Connie gazed at him. Of course. That was the point. Some enemy of Mr Bamberger wanted his guests to become so nervous on the voyage they would talk about it to each other. Dark rumours would spread about the *Princess May* and no one would want to sail on her again.

'Must have been another bellboy, oiling the door,

careless like,' said the boy.

'I don't think so,' said Connie. 'Hang on, don't clean it all off yet.'

Sighing, she pulled out the clean handkerchief that had replaced her stained one since breakfast and dabbed a corner in the oil. The bellboy watched her curiously.

'You see,' said Connie by way of explanation, 'there's been a lot of oil around on this voyage. This is the third hanky I've used to take samples.'

The boy's jaw dropped. 'You mean – it's been spilled deliberate like?'

'I don't know, but it's most mysterious.'

'You a detective, or sommat?' he said, with a grin.

'No, an anthropologist.'

'What's ur anthri-whatever when it's at home?'

Connie gave up. 'What's your name?' She put out her hand. 'Mine's Constance Clementine Carew.'

'Blimey!'

The boy put down the wet cloth and shook her hand. His hand was raw-knuckled and rather slimy from cleaning. 'Bobby. Pleased to meet you, mate.'

Connie found she didn't in the least mind being called 'mate'; in fact, she rather liked it.

'What on earth are those?' she asked, pointing to

what looked like a pair of shoe soles on wheels, parked near his tin bucket.

'I'm a rinker,' he said, with a touch of pride. 'Those are my rollers. Helps me speed around the ship like billy-o! The bell goes and I'm there in a trice. There's a craze for them, you know, back on dry land.' He stuck out his scrawny chest. 'If they hold another championships next year, I might have a go.'

'Are you very good at it?' asked Connie dubiously.

He hesitated, suddenly bashful. 'I reckon I'll need to be a bit better – to win the championships, that is!'

Connie squatted down to examine the roller-skates. They had clever leather straps for fitting around the wearer's shoe. She immediately wanted to try them on herself.

'Perhaps I'll see you again,' she said wistfully, as she stood up.

'You will. This is my passage.' He gave his wide grin. 'All the toffs. Mr Bamberger's specials.'

Connie found Ida sitting on her bed. She looked both quietly furious and as if she had been sitting there a long time.

'Where's Arthur?' said Connie.

Ida shrugged. Even her shoulders looked cross. 'He's going through music sheets with that blooming dancer. We went down to the ballroom because Arthur wanted to rehearse his pieces for tonight and there she was, doing her practising, leaping about, doing funny curtseys and all that.'

'Oh,' said Connie. Suddenly she felt rather guilty.

'Arthur wanted to stay. She put her arm round him, showed him the music she'd brought for the last night when she's to do her dancing. I couldn't drag him away.'

'If Radmilla's dancing *The Dying Swan*, she can't go on dying for ever,' Connie pointed out. 'He'll be back with us for lunch.'

And he would be. Arthur had always loved his food, Connie knew that. She knew that for some years since he had lived in London it had been hard for Arthur as a student to make ends meet. Whenever he had the chance of a decent meal he had tucked in, not that it had made much difference. Arthur had remained slim and elegant, despite his increasingly threadbare clothes.

But he didn't turn up in the first-class dining saloon for a while, then he breezed in with Radmilla,

76

looking pleased with himself.

'Zis is my new discovery!' Radmilla announced, putting her hands on Arthur's shoulders as he sat down. Ida ignored them and continued talking to Biffer Smith. 'He plays like an angel and he will learn ze music I have for him. I will dance even better zan before! It is true I rival the great Pavlova in zis role, like zey say. I take him back to Paris wiv me!'

At this Ida looked up. 'You can't,' she said shortly. 'He belongs to me.'

The prospect of being fought over by two young women was entirely new to Arthur. He looked down shyly and his ears went pink.

Meanwhile, there was a general atmosphere of unease at the luncheon table that was not helped by the slight motion of the ship. Mr Bamberger's guests picked cautiously at their food. Connie heard the words 'yellow overalls', 'heavy footsteps', 'almost broke her back' drifting across the table. Muriel Pope sat speechlessly, eating little. There was no sign of Mrs Cartmell yet, nor of Elmer.

Connie was sitting sandwiched between the two actresses, who chattered across her to each other about their hopes of appearing on Broadway and whether they would become famous in the States. Connie watched their crimson mouths opening and shutting.

Dolores Devine, dark-haired and with kiss-curls on her forehead that looked as if they had been glued on, gazed wistfully at where Biffer Smith was talking to Ida and taking notes, while he kept an admiring eye on Radmilla.

'Biffer interviewed me once, you know, Ver,' she mused, flicking her hair back with her long painted nails. 'I was only fifteen then, a juvenile lead in my first play. Not actual theatre, mind you – a gentlemen's club – but he still called me "promising".'

'That's what he called me when I was seventeen, Dor!' The other actress, blonde, her prettiness spoilt by a small, petulant mouth, looked sourly across the table. 'He's chatting up that heiress now.'

'He's old for the game,' Verina said, with satisfaction. 'Desperate for a scoop, he is.'

They both nodded. 'He's not going to get it on this ship,' said Dolores, tossing her dark hair.

'What about Radmilla whats-her-name and Waldo Bamberger? He hasn't written about that, has he?'

'Waldo asked Biffer not to, apparently. Anyway, it's stale news, Ver. That affair was over ages ago. She was furious, didn't you read about it in the gutter press? Surprised she came on this trip.'

'Oh!' said Connie. She was learning some useful information, even if it was somehow disturbing to think that her Mr Bamberger and Radmilla Oblomov had once been together.

Her neighbours paused mid-mouthful, as if they had just realised she was there.

'I'm Constance Clementine Carew,' Connie said brightly. 'How do you do?'

Verina Vane eyed her doubtfully. 'Some name, kid! You a child actress as well as a chaperone?'

'No,' said Connie. 'I'm myself.'

Louie Leblank breezed over, appearing from nowhere in his usual way. 'How are you all doing, folks?' he said, looking around, a smile cracking his waxen face. 'Enjoying your lunch? And girls? Everything OK?'

'Yes, Mr Leblank,' the two actresses chorused.

Once he had disappeared, Verina Vane hissed at Dolores Devine, 'He's another actor! I'm sure I've seen him in panto!'

'Really, Ver?' Dolores hid a grin behind her hand. Connie said nothing.

Verina nodded her fair curls. 'Weston-Super-Mare years back. Played Buttons in *Cinderella*. Mum took me when I was little. I fancied playing Cinders, of course.'

'But Louie Leblank is American, Miss Vane,' Connie couldn't help saying.

She winked. 'Is he? We all need jobs. He's changed his name, of course.'

'We've all done that, haven't we, Ver?' said Dolores, with a giggle.

'So what are your real names?' asked Connie, fascinated. She would have to alter her notes.

'Swear not to tell anyone?' said Dolores.

Verina leaned closer and whispered in Connie's ear. 'Doris Grubb and Vera Tubby!'

Dolores looked at Connie and made a face. 'See what I mean?'

Connie did.

'We had to change 'em, didn't we? But keep mum about it. You can call us Dor and Ver – much easier.'

Connie wasn't sure whether 'Door' and 'Veer' were an improvement as far as names went, but she nodded.

'Cheery-bye, love,' said Veer, standing up. 'Must be off for a bit of shut-eye. Catch up on beauty sleep. Coming, Dor?'

The two of them stood up and sashayed off, linking arms as they crossed the dining-room floor and laughing as they swayed to the movement of the ship.

Mrs Cartmell flounced in past them, towing a shamefaced Elmer.

She sat down as far away from Connie as she could, which meant she had to sit opposite Ida. Ida glanced at her, raised her chin and looked away deliberately. Clearly she hadn't forgotten how rude Mrs Cartmell had been earlier.

Elmer sat glumly, still rather pale about the gills.

'You silly, silly boy!' Mrs Cartmell exclaimed, in tones that carried around the entire table. 'Stuffing yourself mid-morning like that! No wonder you felt nauseous. You should have stayed with me! No lunch for you!'

'Aw, Marmee,' Elmer began weakly. 'I'm much better—'

She interrupted him. 'No more running off like that again, do you hear? From now on you avoid other children and remain with me.' She gripped the lunch menu as if it were Elmer's shirt collar, then turned to the hovering waiter. 'I'll start with the cold cucumber soup, followed by the roast beef. Nothing for my son.'

'If I might put in a word, my lady,' said the waiter, with utmost politeness. 'Ice cream is generally considered an excellent remedy for seasickness.'

Mrs Cartmell looked flattered at being called 'my

lady'. She hesitated, then nodded reluctantly. A tiny smile crossed Elmer's face.

Connie waited for Ida to finish her peaches in liquor. The waiter arrived with Mrs Cartmell's bowl of soup and a basket of fresh bread rolls. He put the basket down near her plate.

At that moment the ship gave an unexpected lurch. The other passengers at the table watched open-mouthed as the bowl of soup tipped and a wave of chilled, creamy liquid flowed over Mrs Cartmell's substantial front. Her expensive lace-covered bosom turned from a delicate vanilla to a delicate cucumber green.

With a gasp, she rose to her feet, choking in fury. Her eyes blazed, her voice was hoarse.

'You stupid fool! I shall have you fired!'

'My sincere apologies, madam,' said the waiter humbly. 'The motion of the ship took me by surprise. I'll bring you another soup immediately.'

'I don't want another, you idiot! I need to change into clean clothes. It's too bad! I shall complain to Mr Bamberger. What with the oil too!'

'There's no oil in this soup, madam, I do assure you,' said the waiter in offended tones.

'No, you idiot! Outside my cabin this morning.

I might have slipped and broken my leg!'

The waiter looked bewildered but ploughed on. 'Again, I do apologise. Your steward will see to the dry-cleaning. I hope no harm is done.' He paused. 'It *is* very good soup.'

Mrs Cartmell gave a terrific snort, stood up and strode out of the dining-room.

Ida and Arthur exchanged quiet smiles. Ida must have forgiven Arthur, thought Connie in relief. The rest of the table, led by Radmilla, murmured '*oil?*' and looked at each other in a meaningful way.

The waiter brought Elmer his ice cream without a word but as he put it down he winked at Elmer – almost as if he had spilled the soup on purpose.

Elmer shot round the table to Connie and sat down next to her, clutching his bowl of ice cream.

'Any more clues?' he hissed, one eye on the door in case his mother should reappear unexpectedly. He shovelled in some chocolate ice cream hastily. 'That oil was right by my marm's door!'

'I know,' said Connie. 'I think whoever's doing this wants it to be seen. Someone wants to make sure that people won't sail on the *Princess May* again!'

'Really?' said Elmer, his voice squeaking. He caught Connie's pointed stare and blinked. 'Well, it couldn't be my marm. She would have had to put the oil there herself! Anyhow, I thought you suspected Louie Leblank.'

'All Mr Bamberger's guests are suspect from now on – your mother included,' said Connie sternly. 'I'm going to have to investigate everyone.'

After lunch Connie and Ida went to fetch their sunhats. They were halfway down the passage when Bobby came speeding towards them on his roller-skates, carrying a tray of coffee which he had just negotiated with great care from someone's stateroom.

Ida halted. Her hand flew to her mouth.

'*Bobby!* Bobby Sparrow! I never did! Fancy seeing you!'

8

The next moment, not realising he was somewhat precariously balanced on his wheels, Ida had rushed forward and thrown her arms around Bobby. The silver coffee pot, fortunately empty, toppled; the white cup and saucer, manufactured for strong seas, fell but bounced; and both Ida and Bobby collapsed together in a shower of demerara sugar.

'Looks like I'll have to clean up again,' said Bobby, a little glumly, sitting on the gritty passage floor. 'Second time today.'

'Aren't you a tiny bit pleased to see me?' Ida said, pouting.

He grinned. ''Course I am! Cor, haven't we both come up in the world since the Sisters of Hope! You was like a big sister to me there. Whatever are you doing here, girl?'

Connie looked down on them both with mixed

feelings as Ida began to recount her story of finding a family and a fortune. Bobby in turn told Ida how Mr Bamberger had noticed him helping at the garden party in Thurloe Square and offered him escape from the Sisters of Hope in the form of employment.

They looked settled for the afternoon, crouched on the passage floor together. Connie was pleased that Ida was happy, but she *had* found Bobby first. He was her new friend and she wasn't sure she wanted to share him. He also possessed the most enticing footwear she had ever seen.

When Connie had finally managed to extricate Ida, they spent the rest of the afternoon on the promenade deck, playing deck quoits and sliders, in which you had to slide discs into numbered squares with what looked like a gardening hoe.

Arthur was with them: he said he had done all the rehearsing he needed to do for the evening. The ship was still rolling gently and the two of them spent a lot of time giggling and falling against each other while Connie watched in disapproval.

Mrs Pope clapped merrily from the sidelines and

Elmer loitered wistfully until they were both hustled away by a furious Mrs Cartmell.

'Surely you've got something better to do, Muriel! A constitutional round the deck would be good for you. You can keep Elmer and me company!'

Since lunchtime Connie had been mulling over whether she should tell Mr Bamberger what had happened to Radmilla's deckchair that morning and about the oil outside Mrs Cartmell's cabin.

Surely he should know that someone was trying to injure his guests and destroy his ship's reputation? In any case, she had had quite enough of chaperoning for a while.

'I'm going to have tea with Mr Bamberger,' she announced.

Ida and Arthur both looked at her, startled – as if they had forgotten she was there, she thought indignantly. And she had been patiently chaperoning them all afternoon!

'Oh, Connie, do you think you should disturb him?' said Ida. 'He must be so busy.'

'He invited me,' said Connie. 'Before we came he said I could have tea with him whenever I wanted.'

'He didn't necessarily mean it, old girl,' said Arthur kindly. 'That's the sort of vague thing adults say.'

Connie shook her head. 'Not Mr Bamberger. He's never vague.'

And with that, she marched off.

But when she reached Mr Bamberger's stateroom door she paused in disappointment. She could distinctly hear two voices talking inside. Had he asked someone else to tea, too? But what she had to tell Mr Bamberger was urgent and somehow, now she was so near him, it seemed more urgent than it had done at any other point during the afternoon. Perhaps the other person would be tactful and leave. So she lifted her hand to knock.

She was disconcerted when the door opened and out strode Hiram Fink, a frown between his eyes. For a moment he didn't appear to see Connie at all, then he stopped, surveyed her grimly and called back over his shoulder, 'Waldo, you have another visitor – a young lady!'

'Send her right in. Can't keep a lady waiting.'

'See you tomorrow then, Waldo. Here's hoping you'll change your mind.'

Hiram Fink went off with his bulging briefcase and Connie went in.

To her great surprise the stateroom was no grander than the one she shared with Ida, although it had a small dining area off it. Mr Bamberger was seated at the dressing-table but he had adapted it into a desk and it was covered with papers instead of Ida's bottles.

It looked as if he was hard at work. He was in his shirt-sleeves and wearing a pair of spectacles, which made him seem altogether different and stern, so that when Connie faltered, 'You said to come to tea . . .' she couldn't think of anything else to say.

Mr Bamberger stopped looking solemn and his face broke into a smile. 'Why, Connie, so I did!'

Connie recovered her voice. 'I knew you weren't vague,' she said with satisfaction, and settled herself comfortably into one of the two large armchairs.

'We had better order some tea then, hadn't we? I'll press the bell.'

'You look very busy.'

'Busy? I'm always busy! But never too busy to see you. Besides, what I'm doing is boring me stupid.' He pronounced the word 'stoopid' and slapped his knee to emphasise it. 'I'd much rather talk to you, my dear.'

'Oh, good. Because I've an awful lot to tell you.'

He gave a mock frown. 'That sounds serious.'

'It is. Very.'

'Tea first. Then you tell me what's troubling you,'

said Mr Bamberger firmly. 'A proper English tea for two, please,' he said to the bellboy, who had arrived with alacrity and who happened to be Bobby.

Bobby grinned at Connie behind his hand. 'Righto, Mr Bamberger, sir.'

The tea, when a rather grander steward brought it, was magnificent. Scones, jam and cream. Fish paste sandwiches. Iced buns. Victoria sponge as well as fruit cake. Wobbly jelly in little glass bowls.

It took considerable eating.

Mr Bamberger enjoyed it too, apart from the moment during the tea when he talked about his own little girl, whom he had lost at birth, together with his young wife, a few years before. Then his round, fleshy face became long and lugubrious. He pointed a photograph of her out to Connie.

She had a sweet face, Connie thought, as she jumped up to inspect it, with dark hair piled up, and she was wearing a beautiful sweeping robe.

Before Mr Bamberger could become too sad, she told him about her own parents, both archaeologists, who had died of cholera on a dig in Egypt four years ago, but how now she was perfectly happy living with her two beloved aunts.

'Perhaps you'll meet someone else and marry

again,' she said. She didn't like to mention Radmilla, since it seemed that that was all over and they certainly hadn't got married.

'No one will ever replace my wife.' Mr Bamberger smiled a trifle wistfully and looked around. 'But I have a fleet of beautiful ships and a good life. Though sometimes there are hard decisions to make. Like should I sell some of the company to Mr Fink? Do you think I should, Connie?' He leaned back and wiped his mouth with a snowy-white napkin.

'I'm afraid I don't know anything about companies,' Connie said humbly.

She could tell, though, that he wasn't seriously asking her opinion – he was half-teasing her in the way that grown-ups did for their own amusement because he knew she wouldn't know the answer. 'But if I owned the Shining Seas shipping line I wouldn't want to sell any of it to anyone else!'

'Even if it was for a great deal of money and would enable me to build even better ships?'

'Better than the *Princess May*?' Connie frowned and Mr Bamberger laughed.

'Do you really want to win the Blue Riband, Mr Bamberger? I want the voyage to last as long as possible!'

'I rather agree. But it would be an honour to be able to inform your king that we'd broken the speed record.' Mr Bamberger smiled and looked over for a moment at the photograph of his wife, as if he were seeking her agreeement. 'But the captain has to think of safety first on every voyage. Safety for the passengers must come before speed.'

This was the perfect moment for Connie to recount all that had been happening to his guests in the last couple of days. She leaned forward in her armchair and fixed him with earnest eyes. 'That's partly why I'm here, Mr Bamberger.'

'Shoot, then, Connie! What's this "serious" stuff you have to tell me?'

Connie told him. She told him about the spot of oil she had found the night before, about the damaged deckchair that Radmilla had almost sat in, which, too, had been marked with oil, and about how it might have ruined her dancing career for ever if it had collapsed under her.

When she mentioned Radmilla, she watched Mr Bamberger's face very carefully to see how much he still cared about her. Not a flicker passed over his features, though perhaps his eyes narrowed a little.

Then she told him about the oil outside Mrs

Cartmell's cabin. To prove her story, she pulled out her three stained handkerchiefs with their dark corners.

Mr Bamberger considered the hankies gravely as they lay one at a time, looking very small in his large, plump hand.

'You see, I took samples,' said Connie. 'It's all the same oil.'

'So it is,' said Mr Bamberger.

'And Mrs Pope's life-preserver was oily, too. Then there's Ida seeing a ghost and Mrs Pope hearing footsteps all last night.'

'You'd better tell me more,' said Mr Bamberger.

When Connie had finished, Mr Bamberger leaned back in his chair. He did not look as worried as Connie thought he should be. She was dismayed to see that he looked full of tea and cake and considerably relaxed, much more so than when she had first arrived, and even a little amused.

'The thing is, Mr Bamberger, I think that someone is trying to put your guests in danger in order to put the blame on you and the ship. No one will ever want to sail again in the *Princess May* if anything bad happens!'

'Connie, honey,' said Mr Bamberger gently. 'I don't want you to worry your head about this on my account. I grant you, there does seem to be some prankster aboard who is playing tricks with the spilled oil. I shall have hell to pay with Cornelia, I fear, if her skirts have been spoiled! But I can't believe there is any dire motive behind it. It could be one of our bellboys, I'm afraid. They're all young and fond of japes. One may have gone a trifle too far with Radmilla's deckchair, but she didn't have a serious accident, thanks to you.

'As for Ida's ghost – well, we had been talking about the drowned boy at dinner. The same goes for Mrs Pope. She's a nervous sort, given to imaginings, from what little I've seen of her, especially at night-time, I guess.'

'But Ida isn't nervous at all,' said Connie.

'*You* didn't see this ghost, did you?'

'I saw somebody,' said Connie unhappily, 'but—'

'I certainly don't believe in ghosts and it would surprise me very much if you did.'

Mr Bamberger looked seriously at Connie and she could sense that he really meant what he said next. His eyes weren't smiling at all now.

'Listen, honey. I don't want you to trouble yourself with this. People can act strange aboard ship. It's its own little world. Gossip – rumours – spread easily.

Passengers get alarmed. Stuff gets out of proportion. Keep any worries between you and me. Everything we say in here is confidential. OK?'

'OK,' said Connie. The unfamiliar phrase sat uneasily on her tongue but she liked 'confidential', which sounded like secrets. 'Does that mean I can come to tea again?'

'Of course.'

Mr Bamberger smiled, as the ship shifted and the plate with its one remaining iced bun rolled irresistibly towards Connie.

'Glad to see you don't suffer from seasickness, young Connie!'

Of course it was typical of grown-ups that they never took you seriously until something serious actually happened. Even nice Mr Bamberger.

But if she went to tea with him each day, Connie thought, as she left his stateroom, at least she could keep him up to date with events. Shut away, working at his papers, how else was he to know?

Mr Fink wasn't going to tell him, even if he visited Mr Bamberger every day about buying part of the

Shining Seas shipping company. It was doubtful that Hiram Fink noticed anything that wasn't to do with money. She didn't think she liked Mr Fink very much.

It was up to her, Connie Carew, to inform and protect Mr Bamberger. Things were going wrong on board the *Princess May*. She was going to investigate until she discovered exactly who was behind them.

As she went down the passage, she saw Bobby skating ahead and darted after him.

'Bobby!' she hissed. 'I want to ask you something important!'

While Connie watched critically, he tried to show off a perfect half circle on his roller-skates and almost overbalanced. However, with the help of a hand on the passage walls he wobbled round to face her.

'Fire away then, mate. What's up?'

Connie couldn't help being secretly pleased that she was still his mate, despite the recent reappearance of Ida.

'It's this,' she whispered, one eye on a couple who were advancing towards them down the passage. 'Have you noticed that any of the bellboys have had dirty hands? *Oily*, I mean?'

''Course not,' he whispered back indignantly, doing little sideways movements to keep steady. 'Our hands are inspected three times a day by the chief cabin steward! Clean as a whistle, they have to be!'

'Someone is playing jokes on Mr Bamberger's guests. Spilling oil and doing other things.'

'Well, it won't be a bellboy,' said Bobby. 'We want to keep our jobs!'

'All the same, if you do see any of them doing anything suspicious, will you tell me?'

He frowned. 'What sort of suspicious?'

'That's just the trouble. I won't know until it happens.'

9

By the time dinner was over, the sea had calmed and the ship had steadied.

Arthur had played the piano in the intervals between courses in the first-class dining saloon, but the big band was playing down in the ballroom this evening and once dinner was over he was free. He and Ida went arm in arm down to the ballroom, with Connie tagging behind.

Connie was wearing her best Indian muslin and Ida had suggested she put her hair up and lent her a jewelled clasp to decorate it. Connie felt very awkward out of her everyday clothes and with her new hair, even though Mr Bamberger was there and admired her appearance. The Captain was there too, dark-haired and handsome in his gleaming white uniform; he was surrounded by ladies, including Mrs Cartmell, who had become quite fluttery.

It grew late. Connie had been trying to chaperone Ida and Arthur as they danced, but her eyes kept closing as she sat at the table, watching them.

For a while Elmer hovered.

'Would you care for a turn around the floor, Connie?' He gave a hopeful smile.

'Where's your mother?'

'Still talking to the Captain.'

Connie thought of shuffling around the floor with Elmer. It would be so embarrassing. He would tread on her toes, she would tread on his. And horror of horrors, he might rest his immaculately oiled head against hers! He was only her height, after all, even a little smaller. But it pained her to say no when she saw how his face fell.

'But you can sit next to me if you like.'

He sat down quickly before she changed her mind. The band was playing very loudly, which meant they couldn't talk. However, during a brief lull while the band members conferred together about the next number, Elmer whispered to Connie, 'Say, if my mom's a suspect, does that mean I can't help you with clues?'

'There aren't any clues, Elmer,' said Connie. 'I haven't found a single one. Besides, Mr Bamberger is sure it's only one of the bellboys playing jokes. He could be right. I don't know for certain yet.'

Elmer looked relieved about his mother, but disappointed all the same. 'So there's no mystery?'

Connie debated her answer. 'Probably not,' she said at last.

When Elmer began giving enormous yawns, Connie found she couldn't help copying him. He mumbled goodnight eventually and she managed to stay awake for a little while longer, until Ida floated up in her ice blue chiffon.

'Connie, dear. It's very late. What would Aunt Dorothea say?'

At the mention of her aunt, Connie felt an unexpected jolt of homesickness. How was Aunt Dorothea without her? Really, there were just too many people to feel responsible about!

Ida kissed her. 'Me and Arthur will survive without you, you know.'

It was strange the way that Connie suddenly felt wide awake as soon as she had left the heavy, scented atmosphere of the ballroom. When she reached the bridge deck she thought it would be fun to go out and look at the stars instead of going straight to her stateroom. The stars were so brilliant out here, far away from London, where they were often hidden by fog.

It was so late that even the bellboys standing by the doors to the deck must have gone to bed. It was so late that for once there were no romantic couples standing close and gazing into each other's eyes, rather than at the much more interesting sea.

Connie was alone. The stars were glittering like a veil of spangled silk against the great dark dome of the sky as it swept down to meet the waves. She took a deep breath of the wild, salty air and skipped across to the deck rail.

Leaning over, she watched how the ship cut smoothly through the inky black water, leaving a trail of white bubbles, as if the fish somewhere deep beneath had broken up to the surface for a split second and blown them. The wind of the ship's passing blew across her hot face and she felt suddenly exhilarated.

She was free! It was late at night and she was out on deck alone, with no Aunt Dorothea to tell her to go to bed.

It was then that she became aware that she was alone no longer.

The double doors at the far end of the deck had opened and closed. Someone had come out on deck, silently, as if they didn't want to be heard.

For some reason, Connie felt an awful foreboding. She held fast to the deck rail and turned her head. The distant overhead lights glimmered on yellow overalls, on a flat cap that hid whatever was beneath. Then the figure was lost to her sight for a moment as it glided out of the light and into the shadows near the deck rail.

In spite of herself, a shiver ran through her. But she didn't believe in ghosts – did she?

Connie didn't move. She stood silently, her hand clamped to the rail as if frozen to it, her head still turned, watching the darkness where something moved. Her heart was beating uncomfortably fast.

There was no sound now, only the water sliding beneath the ship. For what seemed an age, Connie stood, waiting. Had the ghost dissolved away into the night? She could sense no movement. Where was that spectral figure?

Then all at once she saw a raised arm, darker than the darkness.

Something fell, the light glinting on it as it dropped, though it was too far away to see what it was. She thought she heard a splash as the object hit the water but it might have been a wave breaking against the ship.

Then the figure must have turned away from the deck rail because the next moment she saw a flash of yellow again, then the sound of the doors opening once more. The figure had vanished.

Connie paused only a moment. Then she darted up the deck. She was going to follow the 'ghost', if ghost it was! Surely ghosts would dissolve through doors, not have to open them?

The area in front of the lift was brightly lit but deserted.

Connie stopped and stared around. Which passage to take? There were four that led from the lift landing, each pair opposite the other.

Then down one passage she glimpsed a flash of yellow. She sped after it and saw the distant back of a woman in a yellow evening gown at the far end. A second later and the woman had disappeared into her cabin.

She turned down the parallel passage, passing a series of closed cabin doors. The passage was dimly lit, the electrical lights turned low at night. She walked softly, keeping out of their downward glow.

There was nothing to be seen.

Finally she went back to the lift landing and started

up the passage that led to her own stateroom and those of Mr Bamberger's other guests.

Then she stopped, rooted to the spot.

A figure in yellow was lingering at the far bend, where it looped around to the parallel passage. It looked horribly ghostly, for the lights had the strange effect of making it look taller than it had done on deck and the yellow overalls baggier, as if they clothed only emptiness.

Door blundered out of her stateroom, half-asleep, wearing a flowered wrapper, her dark hair in curl papers. She noticed Connie.

'Something brushed against my door,' she called out and knocked on the neighbouring stateroom. 'Ver? Ver? Did you want me?'

Then she looked around, caught sight of the figure and screamed.

It was a very loud scream. It went on and on, echoing up and down the sleeping passage until everyone woke and doors started to open and alarmed faces peered out.

Connie began to run, her hair falling down from its clasp and her sash flying behind her. Someone had to catch that figure and expose it! It had caused all the misadventures on the *Princess May*. If she could just see the face hidden beneath the cap . . .

But it was already too late. The figure had vanished, seemingly into thin air – but Connie knew it was a trick of the light. It must have slipped round the bend at the end of the passage.

She raced down. She had to avoid the clusters of passengers, all agitatingly talking about what Door had seen. Door still screeched, 'Ghost!' in a hysterical way, her face, slathered in cold cream, looking more ghostly than the ghost itself. Stewards appeared, offering to bring warm, soothing drinks and trying to banish the night-duty bellboys, who were watching the spectacle, open-mouthed and gleeful.

'Send for the ship's doctor!' shouted one gentleman, banging his stick on the floor, as Door's hysterics continued. 'This young lady's in need of sedation!'

'I can't sleep with all this noise,' complained an old lady, popping her head out of her cabin door. 'Whatever's going on? I've never known such a racket and I've travelled first-class all my life!'

Connie took in a blur of faces as she dodged past. There was so much commotion that no one noticed her: grown-ups always ignored children when something important happened that needed urgent discussion.

She reached the bend. Behind her the turmoil continued. In front of her were the utility, stewards' and bellboys' rooms, shadowy in the dimmed light.

There was no sign of any ghostly figure, no sign of anyone at all. Yet the stewards must have seen it as they were summoned out by the passengers' bells. Where could it have hidden?

Connie stopped, breathless. Then a gawky uniformed figure came rolling towards her.

'Heard the rumpus!'

'I'm trying to find the ghost,' explained Connie.

Bobby halted, legs dangerously apart and rocking slightly. 'I've spotted a topping clue!'

'What is it?'

'That!' He pointed to a scrap of yellow material caught in the utility room door.

Connie took hold of it and tugged. It felt harsh between her fingers, like canvas or stiff cotton, and the edges were ragged. It was, most decidedly, of human manufacture and not supernatural at all.

'It's from the overalls the ghost was wearing!' she hissed. 'It may still be hiding in there!'

The utility room door otherwise looked as innocent and normal as any door could look. No sound came from within.

'The ghost is probably inside, lying doggo!' whispered Connie. 'I'm going to open it!'

She took a deep breath and took hold of the handle. She felt slightly sick, even with Bobby there. Her fingers were weak. When she managed to turn it nothing happened. The door remained fast shut.

'It's locked!' She looked at Bobby helplessly.

He shrugged and wobbled. 'That's that, then.'

'What do you mean?'

'Well, the door's locked on the outside, see? So no one could be hiding inside, could they?'

'No, but there might be more clues,' said Connie. She pointed at the piece of yellow material. 'At some point whoever it was wearing these yellow overalls might have hidden in there. Or there might be something incriminating inside. We need to open it, Bobby. You can open it, can't you? Can't you get the key?'

He seemed surprisingly reluctant. 'Difficult. Can't go round unlocking doors at night without permission. It would get me into trouble, it would.'

'But who's going to steal from a utility room?' said Connie, exasperated. 'There's only brushes and mops inside.'

He shook his head. 'All the same, better not, mate.

Sorry and all.'

Connie was at a loss. She looked at the piece of yellow material. 'Well, at least you've found me a clue. If I show it to everyone, they'll know it wasn't a ghost that Door saw.'

Bobby seemed relieved. 'I'd better scoot before I have to run some errand or other. I'll see you—'

Before he could finish, an army of stewards strode round the corner towards them.

'Scarper, you young limb!' said one, not unkindly, to Bobby. 'Long past your bedtime. Up at five thirty tomorrow, mind!'

Bobby rolled off at speed, giving Connie a resigned look over his shoulder.

'Apologies, miss,' the steward said to her. 'Was there something you wanted?'

'Yes, actually,' said Connie. 'I want to show everyone the material that's caught in that door.' She pointed. 'Can you get it out for me?'

The steward tutted. 'What's that doing there? Looks like a bit off a duster. These maids are so careless. Everything must be shipshape on the *Princess May*.'

'It's not a duster—' Connie began. But too late. The steward had stretched out a strong hand and wrenched at it. It came away and he pocketed it smartly. 'I shall dispose of this forthwith. Now young lady, you're sure there's nothing you need?'

'Well, there was,' said Connie, but he looked so in command and so stiffly starched in his white jacket that she found herself uncharacteristically daunted. Without saying anything else, she retreated meekly to the first-class passage, where most of the passengers had disappeared into their staterooms and presumably were drinking the soothing cups of cocoa brought by the stewards.

Door had vanished too, though Connie could hear some wails still coming from inside her stateroom and a deeper voice which presumably belonged to the ship's doctor. Only Elmer was in the passage, hanging around in his nightgown as if he were waiting for her.

'Hi, Connie. Say, that was exciting! A real-live ghost!'

'Ghosts can't be live,' Connie pointed out. 'Anyway, it wasn't really a ghost. Just someone wearing yellow overalls, like that poor drowned boy.' She frowned. 'Where's your mother?'

He looked a little embarrassed. 'In the ballroom still, I think. She was hoping the Captain would dance with her.'

Connie came closer. 'Listen, Elmer. This is really

important. Do you remember which of Mr Bamberger's guests came out of their staterooms when Door screamed?'

'Door?'

'Dolores Devine.'

Elmer rubbed his forehead. 'There was such a muddle of people. I took one look, couldn't see anything interesting anywhere, and went back into my stateroom. I saw Miss Devine in the middle of it all, of course, and lots of stewards and bellboys ...' He looked at her. 'Why is it important?'

'Because whoever was out here couldn't be pretending to be the ghost at the same time,' said Connie patiently. 'Maybe it's easier for you to remember who *wasn't* here.'

'Oh, I see. Well, Marmee wasn't here, because she would have sent me straight back to bed, or Mrs Pope, because I guess it's her job to attend Marmee, nor was Louie Leblank, because he must have still been in the ballroom, and nor was Mr Bamberger or the Captain because they were down there too.'

'But neither of those two would have been pretending to be the ghost,' said Connie in exasperation. 'It's their ship! It's yet another attempt to frighten everyone, don't you see? To make people believe this ship is jinxed.' She wasn't certain that Elmer understood the word, so she added kindly, 'Doomed, that is.'

He nodded, pondered, then was suddenly illuminated. 'I didn't see Mr Fink!'

'He's much too sensible to believe in ghosts,' said Connie. 'He would have stayed inside his stateroom, doing more paperwork, I expect.'

Then she paused.

She remembered Hiram Fink's frowning face that afternoon. He wanted to buy the Shining Seas shipping line from Mr Bamberger. If the value of the *Princess May* went down and the company lost money, then perhaps Mr Bamberger would be more likely to sell.

Could the reason Hiram Fink hadn't appeared just now be because he was the 'ghost'?

The Purser's assistant looked Connie up and down disapprovingly. It was after lunch the next day, Tuesday, and Connie had gone to the Purser's office with Ida and Arthur to find costumes for the fancy dress party on the last night.

'I'm afraid we've nothing in her size,' the Purser's assistant said to Ida over Connie's head. 'We don't cater for children. We expect them to be in bed by the time the party starts.'

'Not Connie,' said Arthur. 'She's an honorary adult, you see.'

The Purser's assistant, a harassed-looking woman with steel grey hair, who did all the typewriting for the Purser on an interesting-looking machine, shook her head. 'There's nothing here that will fit her.'

'Never mind, dearest,' said Ida, putting her arm around Connie. 'We'll make you something that will be just as good.'

All the same, Connie couldn't help feeling the tiniest stab of disappointment and envy as Ida and Arthur carried their costumes back to their staterooms to try on.

Arthur was going as King Neptune and Ida as his queen. Her costume was a column of silk that shimmered like mother-of-pearl, complete with a mermaid's tail, stuck with sequined scales, stitched up the back and half trailing behind in a train. She let down her long fair hair and placed the coronet of shells and coral so that they nestled among the soft curls on her forehead.

'How do I look, Connie?'

'Beautiful,' breathed Connie. She came closer and sniffed. 'You don't smell right, though.'

'What do you mean?' said Ida, alarmed.

'You should smell of salt water and fish, and seaweed and octopus and things like that. Salacia wouldn't have smelled of Guerlain perfume, would she?'

'Who's Salacia?' said Ida.

'You are, of course! King Neptune's wife in Roman mythology.'

Ida shook her head. 'The things you know, Connie.'

'If you'd had a governess like Miss Poots, you would too.'

Ida looked at her thoughtfully. 'You know, Connie, your mum did her best for you. She wanted you to have a good education, so she hired old Pootsie. She knew it was important.'

At that moment Arthur came into the cabin, looking equally magnificent in his dark green robes, though the regal impression was somewhat spoilt by his bashful face beneath the glittering fish-scale headpiece.

'I say, Ida, you look absolutely ripping!'

'Darling Arthur. So do you!'

Connie had had enough of this. 'But what am I going to go as?'

They stopped gazing at each other and gazed at Connie instead.

'I could go as your child!' she said brightly.

Ida blushed and looked doubtfully at Arthur. 'Oh, I don't think that would do at all, Connie. Why, we aren't even married yet!'

'You sound like Aunt Dorothea,' said Connie glumly. 'It would only be for one night.'

'But people might get the wrong idea.'

Arthur pondered. 'What about a sea creature?'

Connie cheered up. 'An *exotic* sea creature.'

So that was decided and they set to work devising Connie's costume.

A round hatbox of Ida's, striped in red and white, and decorated with long fronds ripped from her red flannel petticoat, made an excellent headdress once they remembered to cut eye-holes in the cardboard. Arthur brought in one of his threadbare shirts, which Connie wore over her liberty bodice: it came down to her ankles but hid her black stockings. Ida had several fringed silk scarves in red, blue and green which she draped and pinned round Connie so that streamers of them wafted behind her as she walked.

'Do I look exotic?' asked Connie, her voice muffled by cardboard. She could just about make out Arthur surveying her critically outside the hatbox.

'Very,' he said. 'In fact, you look rather dangerous. If I were a fish, I'd swim away at once.'

'Good,' said Connie. She couldn't see herself properly in the stateroom's mirror but what she could see looked promising. Satisfied, she took off the headdress with relief and untied herself from the scarves.

After that they all put on their ordinary outdoor clothes and went out on to the promenade deck.

It was a chilly, blustery day. The sea was sullen

and grey and even the tops of the waves looked dirty.

They settled themselves down on the deckchairs at the stern, where the deck was more sheltered from the wind by the ship's superstructure, and stewards rushed up to them with rugs. None of Mr Bamberger's other guests had braved the elements today.

Connie opened *The Nicest Girl in the School* and sat back.

Ida soon grew bored with her copy of *Home Chips* and muttered that she was blooming frozen, even though she was sitting the wrong way round again, under the shelter of an awning that ran round to the windward side of the ship. Arthur was trying to mark up a music book but after a while he gave up and stared out to sea, humming a tune to himself. When Connie asked what it was, he said it was the dance of *The Dying Swan*.

'I'm learning it for Radmilla to dance at the party on the last night.'

'That woman!' Ida shouted back, who had somehow heard Arthur.

'She is a very good dancer,' said Arthur mildly.

'Well, she won't need to be very energetic – not if she's dying,' mused Connie. 'But a swan?'

Swans were ethereal and pure. Connie could

imagine Radmilla as something dark and dramatic, like Carabosse, the evil fairy at Sleeping Beauty's christening, dressed in cobwebs of black gauze, not white feathers. Miss Poots had taken her to that particular ballet as a treat when she had unexpectedly excelled herself at maths one term.

'You wait, Connie,' said Arthur. 'Radmilla will transform herself. That's what great ballerinas always do.'

In that case, could Radmilla transform herself into a 'ghost', clad in yellow overalls? If so, she might have sawn through that deckchair herself in order to divert suspicion. She had a motive, after all: revenge. Mr Bamberger hadn't wanted to marry her – although Connie was sure he would have told her in the nicest possible way. But suppose she had been very angry and upset?

Connie found she wasn't concentrating on *The Nicest Girl in the School*. She looked thoughtfully at the glowering sea and it was then that she heard it.

The faintest shriek, from the leeward side of the ship, the more sheltered side.

'What was that?' she said to Arthur but he was far away in his thoughts, oblivious to the cold, and hadn't heard anything.

Connie cast off her rug and jumped to her feet. Ida had heard something too. She left her magazine flapping and they both hurried to investigate. At the same time Hiram Fink appeared on deck from the opposite direction, as if he had been alerted by the muffled shriek as well.

Cornelia Cartmell was somewhere between the three of them, hatless and windswept and clutching the deck rail as if for dear life – which, indeed, turned out to be the case, when they reached her.

'I have been assaulted!' she announced furiously. 'Someone tried to push me overboard! And look where my hat is!'

They all looked. There, riding up and down bravely on the waves like a small ship but fast sinking beneath them, was a cream-coloured hat. 'I was particularly fond of that hat, too!' said Mrs Cartmell. 'It blew off in the struggle.'

'Did you see who pushed you?' asked Connie.

Mrs Cartmell glared at her beneath her dishevelled hair. 'Of course not, you silly child! Otherwise I would have had him apprehended straight away! I couldn't see anything at all. The veil had come off my hat in the wind and wrapped itself round my face. I was completely blind!'

'What happened exactly, Cornelia?' said Hiram Fink.

'I felt this terrifyingly strong hand on my back, pushing me with tremendous force. Though I was struggling with my veil, fortunately I was holding on to the rail with my other hand.'

'What a dreadful shock!' Ida said. 'Would you like to sit down?'

'No, I would not! I am not an invalid.' She took a deep breath. 'Really, this ship! Whatever next? Are we all in danger?' She ignored Ida and Connie and addressed Hiram Fink. 'Hiram!'

Hiram Fink, who had been listening with a frown, leaped to attention. 'Hiram, would you be so good as to take me in to tea?'

Mr Fink looked around. 'Of course, but is your lady companion not around?' he said – hopefully, Connie thought. 'I wouldn't want to usurp her duties.'

'She went off to fetch a coat. She was cold, she said. She never wraps up properly. Besides, I should be glad of a masculine arm. After tea I shall go and report all this to Waldo. He should know there is a would-be murderer on board!'

It was interesting that Hiram Fink had so quickly arrived on the scene, Connie thought; it might be suspicious. She watched him help Mrs Cartmell away. She was leaning heavily on him, her arm tucked firmly into his.

At that moment Muriel Pope hurried up, a woollen coat of a nondescript colour flapping over her skirt. Her usual worried expression grew more worried still when Ida told her what had happened to her employer. She twisted her hands together and shook her head.

'It's all my fault,' she wailed. 'I never should have left her alone! She will blame me.'

'Surely not? It wasn't your fault,' Ida said soothingly.

'But it was, you see! We'd been walking up and down – Mrs Cartmell likes a constitutional in the afternoon – and I'm afraid I became quite chilled through. I had suggested the aft deck out of the wind but she said we should only disturb you and would have a longer walk here. I went to get my coat. I can only have been gone ten minutes or so.'

'Did you see anyone else while you were walking?' Connie asked.

'I saw Mr Fink in the distance. And we passed various other people – none of Mr Bamberger's other guests, though.' She stared at them both, watery-eyed. 'Too dreadful to think someone was trying to drown her!'

'Perhaps you'd better go and rescue Mr Fink,' said Connie. 'He's taken her in to tea.'

'Oh dear, oh dear. Yes, I must.' She gave them both a last agonised look and stumbled away towards the double doors, her head bent against the wind.

'Come on, Connie, it's cold out here,' said Ida. 'Let's go and find Arthur. I wouldn't mind a cuppa myself.'

Something was bothering Connie; she felt uncharacteristically muddled. 'Did you see Mr Fink's face while Mrs Cartmell was telling us what happened?'

Ida shook her head. 'Why?'

'He looked as if he didn't believe her. As if he thought she was making it up.'

But why should he think that if he had been the one who pushed her?

11

When Connie, Ida and Arthur arrived in the first-class tea lounge, Mrs Pope was already busy giving flustered excuses to Mr Fink as to where she had been, and why, during the time her employer had been almost pushed overboard.

Mrs Cartmell sipped her tea and stared impatiently at her companion over the rim of her cup. She was clearly fully recovered. Even her hair, released for a few wild moments, had sprung back into shape.

Connie thought that Mr Fink looked as if he were longing for the explanations to come to an end so that he could leave without appearing rude. Or was it because he feared he might fall under suspicion if they continued?

Very shortly he did leave, passing Connie's table, but gazing straight ahead, as if he hadn't seen the three of them there.

Connie gulped her tea and jumped to her feet. 'There's something I must do. I'll see you later.'

'Where are you going?' Ida called after her but Connie pretended not to hear. She was, of course, on her way to see Mr Bamberger to tell him what had happened, but she knew Ida would think she was bothering him.

As she neared Mr Bamberger's stateroom she was taken aback to see Hiram Fink again, coming out. She retreated further down the passage and waited, and to her relief he disappeared off in the opposite direction without seeing her.

She knocked and Mr Bamberger's voice called out, 'Come in!'

'Connie, my dear! Have you come to have tea with me again? I'll call a bellboy.' He was smiling up at her from his chair by the desk. She hated to make his cheerful, welcoming face sad and anxious.

'That would be lovely,' she said carefully. 'But there is something I want to discuss with you.'

Bobby came and took the order, grinning at Connie.

'Are you two acquainted?' said Mr Bamberger curiously.

Connie nodded. 'We're friends.'

'I'm afraid there aren't many young people aboard.

You must be lonely.'

'I'm not lonely at all,' Connie assured him. 'There's Bobby and there's Elmer Cartmell and my cousin Ida and dearest friend Arthur and you, yourself, Mr Bamberger!'

Mr Bamberger looked pleased to be included amongst such illustrious company, but before he could say anything else, Connie said, 'It's actually about Elmer's mother that I've come to see you.'

At that moment a steward arrived with another magnificent tea. What with managing the teapot and helping herself to jam, cream and scones under Mr Bamberger's beaming smile, it was a little while before Connie could actually say what she had come to say.

'I'm afraid someone tried to push Mrs Cartmell overboard this afternoon!' she burst out. 'She'll be arriving any moment to complain!'

'Then we'd better eat as much as we can before she arrives,' said Mr Bamberger calmly and managed to fit three scones on to his plate at once.

'Mr Bamberger, you don't understand! Mrs Cartmell almost drowned!'

'I know that's what she said. Hiram came and told me. He thought I should know.'

'But aren't you worried? There could be someone on board who's trying to—'

'I'm much more worried about being visited by Mrs Cartmell!' Mr Bamberger leaned forward and patted her knee. 'Don't you worry yourself, Connie. Remember that we agreed that everything we said in here was in confidence – between you and me?'

Connie nodded.

'Well, between you and me, Mrs C likes a bit of attention. She likes to create drama with herself as the heroine. Hiram and I have known her a long time. We supported her when her marriage wasn't going too well. My, there was a lot of drama then! But she's built up a good business since the separation and Elmer's a sensible young man. He'll turn out OK if only she can leave him alone.'

'So you don't think she was telling the truth?'

'Not the whole truth. I think maybe she panicked when her hat veil wrapped itself around her eyes. That bit was true. I think she imagined the hand on her back.'

'She lost her hat, though, and she was fond of it,' said Connie. 'We saw it in the sea.'

'It blew off, just as she said.'

'But everyone will believe her and think there's a

murderer on the loose!'

Mr Bamberger spoke through a mouthful of scone, in a way that Aunt Dorothea would not have approved. 'How many passengers do you think we have on board?'

'I don't know. Lots and lots.'

'Exactly,' said Mr Bamberger comfortably. 'All they will see is a fine ship with excellent service and amenities. What one passenger says up in first-class won't bother 'em.'

'But what about the other first-class passengers?'

Mr Bamberger smiled, as if it was all a joke, as if he wasn't taking it seriously at all. 'You'll just have to reassure them, Connie!'

'But Biffer Smith is writing a diary of the voyage, which will be published in the newspaper!'

'I'll have a word with Biffer. He's been discreet before. That's why I asked him.'

'Oh,' said Connie, disconcerted. She remembered Veer mentioning that Biffer hadn't written about Mr Bamberger and Radmilla.

Before she could say anything more there was a thunderous knocking at the door and a voice shouted, 'Waldo?'

Connie put her hand to her mouth. 'Oh dear.

She's finished her tea and come to complain!'

'I daresay I can cope,' Mr Bamberger said easily. 'Now Connie, off you go, my dear, and don't worry your head about me. Enjoy yourself! Come to tea again and tell me if accidents have happened to any of my other guests!'

The door was opened by a nervous-looking Bobby and Mrs Cartmell stood there, blocking the way out.

Connie managed to squeeze past. 'I'm so glad you're recovered, Mrs Cartmell,' she said in her politest voice, trying not to giggle, as behind Mrs Cartmell's substantial figure Bobby pulled faces at her.

'What's that child doing here, Waldo?' Mrs Cartmell snapped.

'She's been taking tea with me, Cornelia. I take it you are here to do the same. I am popular this afternoon!'

'This is not a social visit, Waldo! I have to tell you . . .'

The rest was lost as she advanced into the room and Bobby shut the door behind her.

'What's all that about?' he hissed. 'Her Majesty's in a right bait.'

Connie pulled him further down the passage, out of

earshot, and told him what had happened that afternoon.

Bobby whistled through his teeth. 'I never! Pity whoever done it didn't succeed in pushing her overboard, eh?'

'Don't! That would have been even worse for Mr Bamberger! If someone had fallen overboard from his new ship—' She faced Bobby. 'The problem is, I can't get him to take any of what's happening seriously. He doesn't seem worried at all.'

Bobby nodded. 'Not a worrier is Mr Bamberger. He expects everything to go smooth-like and for the most part it does. We all do our best to please him. He's a good boss, not one for fussin'. Everyone what works for him has respeck. They don't want nothing to go wrong 'cos then they loses their job, see?'

Connie nodded gravely.

'So it's up to you, Connie Carew, to solve the mystery. You will do that, won't you, mate?'

'Of course,' said Connie firmly.

Before dinner that night, while Ida was sitting before the mirror in their cabin, engaged in the serious task of making herself look even more beautiful for the evening, and the air filled with the sweet scents of creams and powders, Connie opened her notebook. She thought back over what she had learned about Mr Bamberger's guests during the voyage so far.

Then she began to write.

Who wants to destroy the Princess May's reputation?

Suspects:

Louie Leblank – ??spying for Mrs Cartmell's husband (unlikely as he was dismissed?)

Cornelia Cartmell – ??doing it for husband (E.C. says they don't live together any more but perhaps she is trying to win him back) Says someone tried to push her overboard but could be lying

Biffer Smith – desperate for story

Radmilla Oblomov – revenge (Mr Bamberger hasn't married her) ??could she have damaged own deckchair?

Hiram Fink – wants to buy company afterwards

Muriel Pope – dislikes Mrs Cartmell. She could have fetched coat and then pushed CC. (But what about her oily life-preserver?)

Door – saw 'ghost' so unlikely
Veer – slept through 'ghost', she says (??)

Ida, dressed in a striking, cobalt blue beaded gown, stared sympathetically at Connie's notebook. 'What a blooming shame that Miss Poots has given you holiday work to do! But you'd better change for dinner now.'

'Can I borrow your hair decoration again?'

Ida was nodding and Connie was about to unbutton her pinafore, when there was a great knocking on the door.

'Oh, my giddy aunt! There's Arthur already,' said Ida as the banging continued, sounding more impatient.

But it wasn't, when Connie bounded over to open the door.

It was Elmer, white-faced and shaken.

'It's Marmee, Connie,' he said. 'She's disappeared!'

12

Arthur appeared from his stateroom, dressed for dinner in the dashing white tie and tails Ida had bought him for the voyage. 'I say, old chap,' he said kindly. 'What's up? You're creating one heck of a rumpus.'

'It's my marm,' said Elmer miserably. 'She's not in her room. She usually dresses for dinner, then raps on my door opposite when she's ready and we go down together with Mrs Pope. She's never late!'

'Doesn't mean a thing,' said Arthur. 'Perhaps she's having a cocktail somewhere.'

'But it does,' said Elmer. 'You don't understand. She would have told me. She tells me everything now that my father –' he hesitated '– isn't around any more.' He gazed imploringly at them. 'Someone tried to push her overboard this afternoon! Perhaps that person is trying to murder her now!'

'She's probably still with Mr Bamberger,' said

Connie. 'They were going to take tea together when I left them. Maybe instead of tea he gave her a strong drink to recover from her experience and she had to stay to recover from that!'

'Connie,' Arthur said hastily, 'I think we all might go into dinner. I'm sure your mother will join us soon, Elmer.'

'Come with us, Elmer,' said Ida. 'I bet your mum will turn up sooner or later, you wait and see!'

Connie wasn't so sure. Two incidents in quick succession both involving Mrs Cartmell seemed more than random.

She followed the others, still in her pinafore and knee-length everyday dress. She tried not to feel like a schoolgirl, while long gowns swished around her on their way to dinner and heads and necks sparkled with diamonds. She hadn't had time even to brush her hair, but she was certain no self-respecting anthropologist would care about unnecessary things like that.

Mr Bamberger's guests were all assembled at their table in the first-class dining saloon, except for Mrs Cartmell and Mr Bamberger himself. They were surprised to see that Mrs Cartmell wasn't among them and looked at each other questioningly.

132

'Oh dear,' murmured Mrs Pope, as if apologising for her employer. 'It is unlike her to be late for dinner.'

Elmer gazed around desperately, as if hoping that his mother might materialise from under the table, if nowhere else. At last he gave up and sat down between Connie and Ida.

'Cheer up, chick,' Ida said, seizing a menu. 'Look, it's that funny thin soup for starters.'

'You must be starving,' said Connie encouragingly. 'You only had ice cream for lunch!'

'I'm not hungry,' said Elmer. Around the table the other guests, freed from the dominating presence of Mrs Cartmell and her opinions, began to converse loudly while tears gathered in Elmer's eyes.

Connie pushed away her bowl of consommé Celestine. Somehow she didn't feel very hungry either. Under the table she reached for Elmer's hand and squeezed it, while she listened to the conversations going on around her.

'I saw nothing this afternoon,' said Muriel Pope, in a plaintive voice. 'I was collecting my coat, you see. So shocking!'

Was that true? thought Connie.

'Interesting,' said Biffer Smith, pulling his notebook from the breast pocket of his white jacket. 'I'd like to know more, if you'd permit . . .'

'No, I didn't sit out on deck today,' said Hiram Fink, sounding aggrieved as he answered someone's question. 'Far too windy. Papers would have blown about all over the place. I went for a little walk on deck, yes. I was some distance away. I didn't see what happened.'

In her head Connie wrote: *But HF there when Ida and I arrived on the scene. Suspicious?*

'So dramatic ze day has been,' said Radmilla, her eyes gleaming beneath a jewelled Grecian band. 'I vish I could have seen zis ghost!'

Veer nudged Door. 'That would have been something, eh, Dor? Seeing Mrs Cartmell almost pushed overboard by a ghost!'

They giggled behind their hands. They had spent considerable time in the first-class bar before dinner, where they had amused themselves by flirting outrageously with the impressionable young barman. Overhearing Veer's comment, Elmer blinked rapidly and bit his lip.

Connie glared at them both, but they didn't notice. 'It wasn't a ghost,' she said.

'It was a murderer!' quavered Muriel Pope.

'A ghostly murderer?' asked Door, with a shudder.

'Hey, do you think he's doing the dreadful deed now?' said Veer with relish, looking at the empty place at the table. 'Only teasing, Dor!' she added, as her friend grew paler still.

'Don't, Ver! You'll give me nightmares! Besides –' Door lowered her voice and jerked her head in Elmer's direction '– you'll worry the kid.'

'Cheer up, Elmer, worse things happen at sea,' said Veer and burst into hysterical laughter.

'I knew from ze start zis voyage was bad,' Radmilla said thickly.

'I vote we go ahead and order,' Arthur interrupted. 'Mrs Cartmell will join us in due course, I'm sure.'

'Quite right, young man,' said Hiram Fink. 'It's possible Cornelia may be feeling a little unwell after her experience this afternoon and is taking her meal in her room.' He looked around the table with a grim expression, as if he did not believe what he was saying himself.

The other guests nodded hopefully. They were relishing the freedom of being able to speak without Cornelia Cartmell dominating the conversation – although, of course, she still was, since they could talk about nothing else.

'I didn't hear her come into her stateroom to dress

for dinner,' Muriel Pope volunteered. 'I thought at the time it was strange. There was absolute silence next door. She usually tells me when she's coming down.'

Mrs Pope herself looked as if she had thrown on her own dowdy gown in a hurry as usual. Sitting next to Radmilla she seemed like a moth hovering uncertainly beside a glamorous butterfly. Now she gazed around with a fraught expression. 'Should I go and look for her, I wonder?'

Arthur patted her hand. 'No need, Mrs P. She'll be here in a tick, I'll bet.'

Time passed. The guests demolished the fish, entrées, desserts and cheeses and started on the savouries, uninterrupted by the substantial figure of Cornelia Cartmell.

'Your mother had tea with Mr Bamberger,' said Connie, seeing Elmer's face. 'She had a lot to complain about. She's probably only changing now.'

Elmer shook his head and a large tear rolled down his nose.

'I thought you said you didn't like her!' whispered Connie.

'I don't,' he said, with a sniff. 'But she *is* my mother. I don't want anything bad to happen to her, like – like – drowning.' He gulped.

'Tell you what,' said Arthur cheerfully, 'after dinner we'll go and see if your mother's room is still empty, then we'll double-check all the public lounges and bars.'

'I'll come with you,' said Mrs Pope, in a tremulous but brave voice. 'It's my duty, after all. She is my employer.'

'She's probably lost,' Ida said. 'It's so very easy on such a big ship.'

'Not for my mother, it isn't,' said Elmer. 'She's used to a large hotel.'

The meal finished somewhat gloomily. Even Arthur, launching into a toe-tapping rendition of the 'Maple Leaf Rag', couldn't lighten the mood. Meanwhile, Connie watched everyone under cover of the extensive wine list.

The two actresses whispered together, while Biffer Smith flipped the blackly scrawled pages of his green notebook, now slightly dog-eared, as if longing to start a whole new report on the missing Mrs Cartmell and her unfortunate experience that afternoon. Radmilla pouted and rolled her huge dark eyes; Hiram Fink studied the menu, perhaps checking on what he had just eaten, his expression lugubrious; Mrs Pope watched the door of the dining saloon anxiously and scattered cheesy crumbs of Welsh rarebit on the tablecloth.

'Everything OK, folks?' said Louie Leblank, popping up suddenly as he always did. 'Enjoy your dinner?'

Elmer scowled and looked away, forgetting his mother for a moment in his dislike of Leblank. Leblank ruffled his hair in a familiar way and he shrank forward in his chair.

'Why, young Elmer, no appetite tonight? And the *Princess* isn't even rolling, not like yesterday lunchtime! Heard about the cucumber soup!' He laughed spitefully, eyeing the other guests as if inviting them to share the joke at the expense of his ex-employer's wife.

'He's lost his mother,' growled Hiram Fink.

'Oops, that's not good!' He brought his hand to his mouth. 'Wherever can she be?'

A very silly question, thought Connie, since no one could answer it.

'Why are you wearing gloves, Mr Leblank?' she asked. They were white cotton gloves and she had noticed them as soon as Leblank had ruffled Elmer's hair. She had only seen stewards wearing gloves before.

Louie Leblank put his hands behind his back in a strange, almost guilty, gesture. 'Why, how observant you are, Miss Carew! If you must know, I cut myself shaving this morning.'

'Perhaps you should let the ship's doctor see it,' said Connie.

'Perhaps.' His voice was cold.

Connie wrote busily in her head: *Why is Louie Leblank wearing gloves? Is it because he cut himself sawing through Radmilla's deckchair?*

But surely she would have noticed if his hand had been bleeding that first morning?

Hiram Fink rose to his feet. 'A word with you, Mr Leblank,' he said gravely.

Connie pricked up her ears. She heard Mr Fink say, 'usual procedure?' Then the words 'First Officer' and 'sound the alarm', while Biffer Smith fingered his notebook.

She looked around. Everyone else was listening too. They looked at each other in consternation as they heard Hiram Fink say 'man overboard'. In the silence his voice sounded unnecessarily loud. Elmer snuffled into his hanky.

'I say, isn't it a bit soon for all that?' protested Arthur.

Connie wrote some more: *Does Mr Fink want to frighten everyone DELIBERATELY and make them think Mrs C has fallen / been pushed overboard? Is it suspicious?*

Before Elmer could grow more alarmed, Connie jumped up, tugging him with her. 'Come on, let's start searching!'

'If you both go to Mrs C's stateroom, then Ida and I will search the lounges,' said Arthur.

Muriel Pope clutched the table for support and stood up. 'I must come with you, young man. No, really, I insist!'

Is this to show everyone what a loyal companion she is? wrote Connie.

Ida put her hand on Elmer's arm. 'Don't worry, kid.'

He looked back at her and tried to smile.

Connie and Elmer went to Mrs Cartmell's stateroom and listened. There was no sound from inside.

Elmer knocked, then banged loudly on the door. 'I did this before,' he said dolefully. 'I thought she might be asleep. But she's not in there, is she?'

'We should make sure she hasn't collapsed,

or something,' said Connie.

Elmer began to shout through the door. 'Ma-arm? Mar-mee?'

Bobby Sparrow rolled up on his skates, alerted by the noise, and executed a juddering turn to bring himself to a stop. 'What's going on?' he asked, his eyes shining with excitement under his thatch of sandy hair, his pill-box hat askew.

'Mrs Cartmell didn't come to dinner,' explained Connie. 'Can you let us into her stateroom – she may be unconscious in there!'

'Lawks!' said Bobby, his face aghast. 'Let you into the dragon's den? Not sure if I dare!'

He saw Connie's glare and said hurriedly to Elmer, 'Apologies, sir. I'll see what I can do.' He fished out his keys, jangled through them and found the right one.

Once they were inside it was clear no one had changed for dinner there, or had even had a lie-down before dinner. The sheet was immaculately turned back, the pillows plumped, the bed smoothed, waiting for its occupant's return.

Cornelia Cartmell was an extremely tidy person, Connie noticed: there were no clothes thrown in happy abandon over the chair, as was Ida's habit in their own stateroom, and the few bottles on the dressing-table were in a regimented row, as if they didn't dare step out of line. The only personal possessions Connie could see were a photograph of a chubby toddler, wearing a smocked dress with baggy trousers, and a pile of books on the bedside table. She glanced at them quickly.

LOVE BENEATH THE LILACS
THE HEART KNOWS ALL
A ROMANTIC IN ROME
NO LOVE FOR LYDIA

Elmer blushed when he saw the photograph, but seemed gratified rather than sheepish. 'Gee, that's me!' Then he looked around forlornly. 'Well, she's not here, is she?'

'Better get out quick, then,' said Bobby uneasily. 'She might come back any minute.'

'I wish she would,' said Elmer. 'What should we do now, Connie?'

'The last person who saw your mother –' Connie was going to add 'alive' but stopped herself in time '– was Mr Bamberger, so we must go and ask him.'

Bobby whistled. 'The big boss? But I've just ordered him his dinner. He's having it with the Purser tonight. You can't interrupt them!'

'We must,' said Connie severely. 'This is an emergency, Bobby!'

'Lead on then, mate,' he said. 'Rather you than me!'

13

Connie led the way up the passage towards Mr Bamberger's stateroom. Bobby slowed himself down so that he could hang back behind the others by clutching at the walls; although determined, Elmer looked distinctly nervous. Even Connie knew it wasn't the right time to visit.

And indeed it wasn't. 'Come,' said an irritated voice that didn't belong to Mr Bamberger, when Connie knocked on the door.

'I can't,' she said, for Bobby was busy taking off his roller-skates and muttering, 'Mark of respeck,' to himself. 'Could you let us in, please?'

It was the Purser who opened it, clearly expecting a trolley-pushing steward with dinner. His hopeful expression vanished and he looked the three of them up and down with raised eyebrows: Connie in her pinafore and day dress, Elmer, with his tear-stained cheeks, and Bobby, crouched on the passage floor undoing his skates.

He cleared his throat. 'Ahem – three children, Mr Bamberger,' he said over his shoulder.

Waldo Bamberger was sitting in the dining area beyond, a glass of bourbon in his hand. The table was set for two, but so far there was only silver cutlery and glass on the white cloth. There was no sign of Mrs Cartmell.

'Tell them to come in,' said Mr Bamberger, putting down his glass. Connie thought she detected a slight note of weariness in his voice. She could tell he wasn't quite as pleased to see her as he had been at teatime.

'I'm sorry to bother you, Mr Bamberger,' she said, as she stepped further into the room. 'But Mrs Cartmell is missing. She didn't come to dinner and she isn't in her stateroom.'

'Connie, I thought I told you—'

'But she could be in danger!'

Mr Bamberger looked from her earnest face to Elmer's woebegone one. 'So you're worried, sonny?' he said, more gently.

'Yes, sir,' said Elmer, in a subdued voice. 'I wondered if she told you where she was going when she left you?'

Mr Bamberger sighed. 'I guess to change for dinner. She left at about half past five this afternoon. I'd given her a cup of tea and heard all about her shock this afternoon.' He glanced at the Purser meaningfully.

'But she didn't,' explained Connie, 'change for dinner. She never went back to her stateroom!'

Mr Bamberger looked at the three of them. 'So you're the search party, are you? Then no need to sound the alarm yet, I think. She's probably in one of the lounges. With young Mr Sparrow's speedy skates, you'll find her in a jiffy, I'm sure.'

Bobby looked oddly ill at ease at the mention of his name, Connie thought. Mr Bamberger must have thought so too, because he studied him more closely.

'I take it you haven't seen – or heard – Mrs Cartmell on this deck this evening, Mr Sparrow? She has a fine, carrying voice.' Here the Purser turned away to cough discreetly into a large handkerchief. 'You haven't answered her bell, by any chance?'

'No, sir, but . . .'

'Is anything the matter, Mr Sparrow?'

Bobby had gone very red and was shuffling about on the carpet.

'I did hear something earlier, sir,' he admitted at last. 'I didn't think anything of it at the time,

146

but now it's come back to me.'

'Like that, has it? Out with it then, young man!'

'There were strange noises coming from –' he hesitated, while four pairs of eyes stared at him '– the utility room!'

With a regretful look at his unfinished bourbon, Mr Bamberger rose to his feet. 'In that case, I think we'd better investigate the utility room, Mister Purser, don't you? Otherwise we shan't enjoy our dinner when it comes.'

'Indeed, Mr Bamberger.'

'Lead on, Mr Sparrow!'

'Why didn't you tell us about these noises before?' Connie hissed crossly at Bobby as the little group emerged from Mr Bamberger's stateroom. 'Perhaps she's shut in there and can't get out!'

She hurried along beside him, with Elmer close behind, while Mr Bamberger and the Purser followed more slowly.

He whispered, 'Because there's an ogre in there, that's why! I was too scared to open the door!'

'An ogre?' said Connie, astonished. 'You're making that up! Don't talk rot!'

Before he could answer they were almost run over by a steward, appearing round the corner with a laden trolley. He looked mortified when he saw Mr Bamberger.

'Oh, sir! Apologies, sir! I was coming as quickly—'

There were explanations behind them as they reached the utility room. Almost simultaneously, Arthur and Ida, accompanied in their wake by a rather breathless Mrs Pope, appeared from the other end of the passage.

'So sorry, old chap,' said Arthur to Elmer. 'Just coming to find you. We've searched where we can, but your mater could be anywhere.'

Elmer gave a wail of despair. 'Marm!'

'There, there,' said Mrs Pope, giving him a clumsy pat on the arm.

There had been silence behind the utility room door, then all at once there was a tiny sound from inside, like the scrabbling of a mouse.

'Hurry, Bobby!' cried Connie. 'Unlock it!'

Bobby pulled out a key, fumbled at the door and turned to them. 'Anyone else want to see what's inside?' he said nervously. He had gone redder than ever.

'Don't be silly! It's not a what, it's a who,' said Connie. 'I bet it's Mrs Cartmell!'

Elmer pushed Bobby aside and put his hand

on the door handle. 'Marm?' his voice squeaked hopefully.

By this time a group of stewards had come out of the stewards' room to see what all the fuss was about. 'What's going on, children?' said one of them. 'Leave that door alone! You can't play in there!'

'Bobby Sparrow, is this one of your games?' demanded another. 'I've told you before not to mess about when you should be working!'

'We're looking for a passenger,' said Connie indignantly. 'She's missing.'

'She'll hardly be in the utility room, miss.'

'But she is in there! Listen!' But now there was no sound at all.

The stewards fell back respectfully for a moment as Mr Bamberger and the Purser approached, like royalty.

'It's OK, stewards,' said Mr Bamberger. 'I am aware of what's going on.'

'Go on, Elmer!' whispered Connie. 'Open it quickly, otherwise they'll lock it again!'

He looked worried. 'If it is a mouse, perhaps it'll run out!'

'Don't be such a baby! It may be your mother!' A whole lot more frightening, in fact, Connie thought.

'A mouse?' said Ida carelessly. 'Don't mind 'em. Plenty of mice in the Home.'

'Mice?' stammered Mrs Pope. 'Oh dear, oh dear!'

Door and Veer were passing, on their way back from the ballroom.

'Mice?' squealed Door, lifting her skirts in horror. Looking around in vain for a chair to stand on, she wrenched the dinner trolley away from the surprised steward and stood gripping it, ready to jump on board among the dishes of roast beef and vegetables. Veer, made of sterner stuff, surveyed the scene inquisitively, hands on hips, and waited.

Watched by the crowd, Elmer bit his lip and turned the door handle.

Behind him heads peered closer and there was a collective gasp of horror.

From the darkness inside the small windowless room a pale face looked out at them. Mrs Cartmell was crouched in the far corner amongst the brooms, brushes and bottles, still in her tea gown, now sadly crushed, as indeed was her hairstyle for the second time that day and everything else about her. She rose stiffly to a bent position, took a few steps towards the open doorway and collapsed against Elmer, her arms in a stranglehold around his neck.

150

'You saved me, my darling boy! I knew you would come!'

'Fetch the ship's doctor,' Mr Bamberger said curtly to Bobby.

Bobby strapped his roller-skates on in an instant and was off, his lanky figure wheeling unsteadily down the passageway; he looked altogether relieved to leave the scene.

Meanwhile, several hands laid Mrs Cartmell out gingerly on the floor and Arthur proffered his precious white dinner jacket as a cushion for her head. She gazed up tearfully at Elmer, who held her hand and stroked it. She ignored Muriel Pope, who was wringing her hands in agitation.

'There, Marmee,' said Elmer softly. 'What happened? How come you were in there?'

That was what everyone wanted to know. They craned closer, while the smell of roast beef and potatoes wafted strongly over them from the trolley.

'Someone pushed me in!' Cornelia Cartmell said in a hoarse voice, but with a trace of her old outrage. 'I felt the very same hand on my back as I had done earlier and then I was inside and I couldn't get out! If it hadn't been for my son, I might have died in there!'

'Aw shucks, Marmee!' said Elmer, pink with

pleasure and amazed pride in himself.

'Was the door already open then?' said Connie.

For a moment Mrs Cartmell's eyes flicked towards her. 'It must have been,' she quavered. 'I was suddenly alone in the darkness! I'd been in there for hours and hours before my brave Elmer rescued me.'

'Did you see your assailant?' asked the Purser.

'Oh, I did! I managed to turn my head as I was pushed inside. I saw a huge strong figure wearing yellow overalls!'

Door put her hand to her mouth. 'The ghost!' she breathed.

'That doesn't sound like a ghost, Miss Devine,' said the Purser.

'All too human, I think, Mister Purser,' said Mr Bamberger. 'Poor Cornelia. What an unpleasant trick to play on you.'

Mrs Cartmell's eyes could still look fierce. 'A trick? This was something more than a mere trick, I think, Waldo! I could have been in there all night and most of tomorrow, until a maid needed an extra brush or another tin of Gumption powder! I could have been in there for days on end and starved to death! It was no trick!'

'Don't agitate yourself so, ma'am,' said the ship's

doctor, appearing through the crowd, followed by a gawping Bobby. The doctor knelt down and felt Mrs Cartmell's pulse. 'I'll give her something to calm her,' he murmured to Mr Bamberger. 'An evening in bed will do the trick, I think.'

It was a most unfortunate word to use again in the circumstances. Mrs Cartmell groaned and closed her eyes. From between her lips came a hoarse whisper. 'Food is what I need, not a sedative. I am absolutely starving!'

'Steward, take that trolley to Mrs Cartmell's stateroom!' Mr Bamberger announced, in a grand sacrificial gesture. 'Her need is greater than ours, eh, Mister Purser?'

The Purser nodded glumly as his long-awaited evening meal vanished out of sight.

Another trolley was fetched from the stewards' room, empty this time, and Mrs Cartmell was laid out on the top.

Shipboard trolleys are built sturdily to withstand the worst weather. Though it protested a little, it was wheeled away with its formidable burden to Mrs Cartmell's stateroom, followed by Elmer, who had rapidly adjusted to his new role as saviour, then by Mrs Pope fluttering after him, and finally by a whole procession of inquisitive onlookers – for by this time many female passengers were returning to their cabins to repair themselves after the early evening's entertainment.

Connie looked around for Bobby but so, it seemed, was Mr Bamberger, and it was Mr Bamberger who caught him first, as Bobby, holding his roller skates, was about to disappear into the bellboys' room.

'Now, young Mr Sparrow,' he said sternly, holding the startled Bobby by the collar. 'Not so fast!'

'Yes, Mr Bamberger?' stuttered Bobby, blinking up at him. 'Is there something I can get you?'

'The truth,' said Mr Bamberger. 'That is what I want from you. Did you push Mrs Cartmell into that utility room?'

'No, sir, I never!' said Bobby, sounding aggrieved. 'Wouldn't dare touch the old—' He bit his lip.

Mr Bamberger gazed at him until Bobby's eyes fell. 'If I find that you have been up to your old ways and are behind all these pranks, Sparrow,' said Mr Bamberger heavily, 'you will be dismissed from this job at once and your roller-skates will be confiscated, do you understand?'

Bobby clutched them protectively. 'Yes, Mr Bamberger,' he whispered. 'It wasn't me, honest!'

'I would like to believe you,' said Mr Bamberger and he let Bobby go. His face, as he walked away past Connie, had fallen into plump folds of sadness. He didn't look at her.

Connie ran after him and tugged at his sleeve. 'Please, Mr Bamberger! Please don't suspect Bobby! I'm sure it's not him.'

Mr Bamberger continued walking. 'Let go of my sleeve, Connie,' he said quietly. 'Bobby has a past history as a practical joker. I know you want to protect your friend, but this has gotten nothing to do with you.'

Oh, but it has! Connie cried inside, but she released his sleeve and watched his back view miserably until it vanished out of sight. Who else would allay Mr Bamberger's suspicions about Bobby?

Only herself, when she found the real culprit.

She ran back to Bobby, full of questions. He gave her an agonised look. 'Can't talk now, mate,' he said shortly and disappeared with alacrity into the bellboys' room.

'Botheration!' Connie said to herself and went to her stateroom to write up her notes.

There was a dreadfully heavy feeling in her chest. The horrid thing was that now she was beginning to doubt Bobby a little, too – at least enough to feel she should record his name in her notebook. He'd looked so very guilty. Perhaps Mr Bamberger had been right from the beginning: perhaps all the alarms on the *Princess May* were merely pranks played by Bobby, with one of them – Radmilla's deckchair – going rather further than he intended. He was tall, like the spectral figure; he'd be able to get hold of oil and workmen's overalls without any difficulty and he evidently had been in trouble before.

So Connie sat on her bed, which, as always, had been pulled down and beautifully smoothed out and even had a wrapped piece of butterscotch waiting for her on the pillow, and reluctantly wrote Bobby's name in her notebook as she sucked the butterscotch.

Bobby Sparrow, bellboy
Character: mischievous, friendly. TRUTHFUL???
(Ogre in cupboard!!)
Motive: practical jokes?

But then she threw down the notebook. She was betraying their friendship with her doubts. Why on earth would Bobby risk losing his job for the sake of a few misjudged pranks?

156

14

'What I need to do,' Connie said to herself when she awoke the next morning, 'is to find some incriminating evidence. Something that will show me who the true culprit is and eliminate Bobby.'

'Eliminate' was a good word; and the phrase, 'incriminating evidence', even better, sounding like something official crime investigators might use. Quietly, so as not to wake Ida, she withdrew her notebook and pencil from under her pillow and wrote:

Incriminating evidence: ?tin of oil / ?yellow overalls

There was one possible place where that kind of evidence might be found: in a stateroom belonging to one of Mr Bamberger's guests. Somehow she had to get into them and investigate.

The ship was steady under her feet, only the faintest vibration under her toes. She dressed as silently as she could, but nothing seemed to disturb Ida, who slept with a beatific smile on her face, probably dreaming of Arthur.

Outside in the passage, the doors were shut fast. It was still early and no one was about, not a bellboy in sight, only a solitary steward pushing a trolley laden with plates of bacon and eggs and gleaming silver racks of toast.

While Connie was eating breakfast at the guests' table, Muriel Pope turned up with her tapestry reticule.

'I like to do Mrs Cartmell's mending first thing,' she said, as she sat down next to Connie and laid the bag on the floor. 'It's so peaceful out on deck with no one else around. So glad to see you're an early bird, too, my dear. Sometimes it's lonely, eating by oneself.'

'You must have had to do that a lot,' said Connie sympathetically. 'Since your husband ran off, I mean.'

'Oh, I have.' A haunted expression crossed Mrs Pope's face and lingered there even after her breakfast arrived. 'Sometimes it's been difficult, indeed. I thought I'd enjoy my first voyage at sea, but all these disasters! First me, then Radmilla and then Mrs Cartmell!'

'How is Mrs Cartmell this morning?' Connie asked politely.

'Right as rain, I think. She was ordering breakfast when I left. My cabin adjoins hers. I hear everything through the door.' She sighed.

'Have you heard the footsteps outside again?'

'Oh, yes. But I'm never sure if it's a dream or not.' Muriel Pope unpeeled the top of her boiled egg, leaving crushed shell spattered round her plate. 'Those sleeping pills from the doctor are strong. I've been taking them since the first night. Of course, Mrs Cartmell doesn't hear a thing.' She leaned towards Connie in a confidential way and whispered, 'She snores!' Then she put her hand to her mouth as if she had said the most outrageous thing.

Connie smiled and suddenly Muriel Pope smiled back.

'I never had a daughter,' she said. 'But a child is a most precious thing. Husbands come and go, as mine did. But a child will be everything to you. You take care, Connie, and choose your husband wisely.'

Connie nodded, although all that was so far in the future, she couldn't even think about it. She wasn't sure that a husband would be at all necessary to an anthropologist.

'Excuse me, Mrs Pope. I must go and wake Ida otherwise she'll sleep right through breakfast!'

As she left, Connie was glad to see Hiram Fink arrive, holding a copy of the ship's newspaper before his face like a shield. So Mrs Pope would have some company. Door and Veer also barged in, made up to their arched and darkened eyebrows and chattering so hard that they almost cannoned into Connie.

Looking back, Connie saw Hiram Fink hesitate, then sit as far away from them as he possibly could without appearing rude. That meant that for courtesy's sake he was forced to sit next to Muriel Pope, since Door and Veer were avoiding her.

Connie smiled to herself. He wouldn't have a chance to read the ship's newspaper this morning, next to Mrs Pope. It seemed she liked to unburden herself to anyone who would listen, even if it was only a twelve-year-old girl.

She must be very lonely, thought Connie, and her heart went out to her because she, too, had once been lonely but now she wasn't, any more.

As she came to the lift the doors opened and she was almost knocked down by the burly emerging figure of Biffer Smith. He looked thunderous and her heart jumped as she saw that the thunderous expression was directed at her. He was, as ever, clutching the green notebook, now more battered than ever.

'Have you been in my stateroom, Miss Carew?' he demanded. He looked positively threatening, his boxer's face jutting into hers and his breath fiery with cigarette smoke.

Connie, struck dumb with shock, felt herself blush. Did he know what she was planning? She shook her head.

'Well, someone has,' he said furiously. 'Look at this, girl!' and he flapped the notebook at her.

Connie gazed at it, nonplussed.

'Some of my notes have been cut from it!' he said impatiently. 'My account of the first dinner, conversations, that sort of thing. Must have happened when I was out on deck early this morning.'

It was true, when Connie examined it closer, that about three pages almost at the beginning looked as if they had been neatly cut out, so neatly that only the owner would know they were missing.

Biffer Smith glowered at her. 'If it wasn't you, then it must have been the boy, Elmer!'

Connie found her voice. 'Why do you think it's either of us?'

'Because children like playing jokes, don't they?' he spat out. 'It's what children do!'

Connie drew herself up and looked him in the eye.

'Not this one, Mr Smith. I take wanton destruction very seriously indeed. I rather think Elmer does, too.'

He looked disconcerted for a moment and his voice softened. 'All right, I believe you.'

'Thank you,' said Connie graciously, and she watched him stump off to confront his fellow breakfast guests.

He had seemed genuinely angry and surely he wouldn't destroy his own notes when he wanted a story so badly? It meant that she could probably cross him off as a suspect.

Along the first-class passage, doors were opening as passengers came out to go to breakfast.

Connie peered in as she passed. None was quite as grand as the staterooms occupied by Mr Bamberger's special guests, but they were impressive all the same.

Stewards were already cleaning the vacated cabins, rushing in and out with dusters and dustpans and brushes. There was a sharp smell of Jeyes Fluid in the air. When Connie came to the staterooms occupied by Mr Bamberger's guests, she hesitated.

A tempting sight was in front of her.

The door to Veer's stateroom was open and she couldn't see a steward inside.

She looked around: no one was watching. She tiptoed swiftly into the room, pulling the door to behind her.

It reminded her immediately of her own, for the mess in there was just like Ida's: stockings dangling over chairs, bottles strewn all over the dressing-table together with half-open lipsticks, magazines by the bedside, a silken nightdress and garish velvet robe in a tangle together at the bottom of the unmade bed. The air was scented heavily with something sweet but nasty and the peardrops smell of nail varnish. The gown that Veer was wearing the night before hung limply from a hanger on the wardrobe door. Without Veer to fill it out, it looked somehow tawdry.

Connie felt horribly nosey as she poked about, lifting up a delicate silk stocking to see what was hidden beneath on the chair seat (only a cushion, disappointingly) – but told herself that all detectives felt this when they were carrying out a vital investigation.

When she peered past the shared bathroom into Door's adjoining room, she could see that it was in very much the same state, with the addition of a moth-eaten teddy bear on the pillow. Door wasn't a suspect anyway, because Connie had been there when Door had seen the 'ghost'.

Somehow yellow overalls and a tin of black oil would be very alien masculine things to find in either room.

Veer could be malicious but it didn't mean she was behind all these nasty events. In any case, what would Veer's motive be in discrediting Mr Bamberger, who, after all, was sending her and Door on their longed-for voyage to fame and fortune?

Connie was suddenly ashamed of her own trepidation and about to fly out as quickly as she came in, when there was the click of the closed bathroom door opening and someone emerged with a bucket and mop. It was a stewardess, young and flustered-looking.

They stared at each other, equally startled.

'Beg pardon, miss,' said the stewardess. 'I didn't hear you come in. I haven't got round to doin' the rooms yet, only the bathroom.'

Connie recovered quickly. 'That's quite all right,' she said grandly. 'Take your time. I'll come back.'

She backed out and continued down the passage, her heart beating hard. But she couldn't help giggling to herself at the thought of the stewardess thinking all those grown-up clothes belonged to her.

Safely back in her own stateroom she crossed off the names Verina Vane and Dolores Devine in her notebook and, after reflection, Biffer Smith's. She was making progress!

All the same, she would have to be more careful the next time she entered a suspect's room.

15

Ida had risen at last and gone to breakfast. Connie waited for her return for a while, grew bored and decided to find her to discuss their plans for the morning.

Walking along the passage to the lift she saw that the door to Hiram Fink's stateroom was open. There was no steward inside. Hiram Fink himself must be still at breakfast.

A tin bucket containing a bottle of Jeyes and a mop sat waiting by the open door, as if the steward had left to find some more cleaning things. Perhaps he or she had run out of Radium Spray and had to fetch it from the utility room, thought Connie, who until yesterday's rescue of Mrs Cartmell had known nothing about household cleaners. It would take the steward a little time to search the room's dark recesses and return.

Time for her to investigate Hiram Fink's stateroom and see if there was any incriminating evidence in there. She hadn't expected the next opportunity to happen so quickly but now that it had, she couldn't waste it.

After all, Hiram Fink was one of her chief suspects. His clever, complex, mournful face looked as if it harboured secrets. He was a gruff and growly man who clearly liked children even less than Biffer Smith did; in fact, he didn't seem to like anyone at all on the *Princess May*. He wanted to buy up the Shining Seas shipping line and he would discredit and bankrupt poor Mr Bamberger to do so.

Connie, exhilarated by her earlier success, strolled in as if Hiram Fink's stateroom belonged to her. Once inside, she pushed the door so that she was hidden from view from outside and began a swift investigation.

After the actresses' rooms, it was remarkably tidy and ordered, almost as if the steward had been busy already, but rather more to do with how Hiram Fink liked his world to be.

There was a pile of old newspapers on the desk in the corner with a note on top that said **PLEASE DO NOT TOUCH OR REMOVE** in thick, forbidding letters. She lifted the pile to peer underneath and several sheets scattered to the floor. Hastily she picked them up and slid them into the bottom of the pile. They would be in the wrong order and crumpled, but Mr Fink would probably never notice.

The bed was neatly folded back, with a pair of striped pyjamas still in their ironed folds on the pillow; all other clothes had been put away and there was nothing on any of the chairs, even on the big armchair. There was a safe on the wall but when she ran to it, it was locked.

On the bedside table there wasn't any soothing reading, only a copy of a book called *Market Swings 1908–1909*, which was certainly not about the kind of swings Connie still secretly enjoyed, and looked immensely boring.

But there was something else.

A photograph on the bedside table, next to the book and a clock and a half-drunk glass of water. It was a copy of the photograph Connie had seen in Mr Bamberger's stateroom: the same dark-haired young woman, smiling out from the leather frame, beautiful and serene. Why should Hiram Fink have a photograph of Mr Bamberger's wife on his table?

There was no time to think properly. Connie continued searching, frantic now. The steward could return any moment.

She opened the wardrobe doors: nothing. She peered into the bathroom and saw only a shaving knife, a pair of nail scissors, a tin of tooth powder and a bottle of Parker's hair balsam.

Back in the stateroom she stared at the desk. On top there was a much-splattered blotter, an inkwell and several pens, their ends chewed. She pulled open the desk drawer. Inside were papers covered with figures in Hiram Fink's emphatic handwriting and when she burrowed beneath these she touched something else.

A gun.

Connie had never seen a gun before. It was small and very black and very evil. She didn't dare touch it in case she shot herself by accident.

She stared, mesmerised, at its solid barrel, at the delicate and vicious trigger that Mr Fink was going to pull to shoot – *who?* Her heart was thumping so hard she thought she would faint.

It was then that she heard raised voices outside the half-closed stateroom door.

Mr Fink had finished his breakfast and returned, only to find a stewardess – not a steward, realised Connie – on the threshold of his room. She had come back with whatever she had gone to fetch. Mr Fink was shouting at the stewardess that he didn't need his room cleaning and she was protesting that it was 'orders from First-class Bedrooms, sir'.

'You can throw your orders overboard for all I care, and the Bedrooms steward too!' said Hiram Fink. 'I need privacy.'

Connie shut the desk drawer as quietly as she could, but in her haste she jerked it and the gun slid heavily over to the other side of the drawer, making a horrible rasping sound on the wood. For a second she thought a bullet might come shooting out and jumped back in horror; but instead, it was the maid who shot in to collect her bucket and mop and Mr Fink who came in after her.

They both stopped and stared, open-mouthed, at Connie. It might have been funny if she hadn't been so petrified.

She couldn't think what to say. She put her shaking hands behind her back, as if somehow they would give away the fact that she had been searching through Mr Fink's possessions.

'You again, miss?' said the stewardess, in a puzzled but accusatory tone.

It was the same stewardess, Connie realised, who had thought earlier that Veer's stateroom belonged to her. The stewardess frowned as she picked up her bucket and shook her head. This was her first position and the habits of some of the first-class passengers struck her as decidedly odd.

Meanwhile, Hiram Fink stood glowering uneasily at Connie. He seemed to be searching for words. They never came easily to him at the best of times, and this, Connie realised, was the very worst.

'Miss Carew!' he said loudly at last. 'What on earth are you doing here? You're trespassing!'

Connie's hands tightened behind her back and she hung her head.

'I'm very sorry, Mr Fink,' she said humbly. 'I'm afraid I mistook your stateroom for the one I share with my cousin Ida. It's only a little way along, you see. I didn't realise my mistake until I'd come in and was going to the bathroom to clean my teeth.'

Mr Fink narrowed his eyes and grunted. He shooed the stewardess out with impatient hands and when they were alone, he frowned at Connie.

'Well, now you're here,' he said, 'would you like me

to teach you about stocks and shares? You seem an intelligent little thing.'

There was a gleam in his eyes. His face lightened as he waited for her answer and for a moment he looked quite different: like a wise and friendly uncle, or a godfather. But someone who kept a gun in his desk drawer was not in the least friendly.

'We could have cocoa at elevenses,' he added, as if to tempt her.

Connie hadn't quite stopped trembling. She thought of sitting in there with Mr Fink for hours and hours, perhaps at the very desk where the gun was hidden, wondering who he was going to murder. It might even be her, if she wasn't very clever at learning about stocks and shares.

'It's very kind of you,' she said carefully, 'but in actual fact I'm going to be an anthropologist when I grow up, not a stockbroker. You see, I don't really want to make money.' She thought of poor Aunt Dorothea, who had had such financial problems before Uncle Harold died. 'It only brings trouble.'

There was a pause. 'How right you are,' said Mr Fink. 'I can see I was correct in my assessment of you, Miss Carew. Well, I shall have to take elevenses on my own, shan't I?'

With that he held his stateroom door open and bowed her out. Connie left, with a crooked smile and trembling legs. She just managed not to run.

16

Connie went and sat in the ship's library.

It seemed a good place to recover, being quiet and peaceful and almost empty. She didn't think Hiram Fink would come after her, but she was still shaking. The ship suddenly seemed small and dangerous, with nowhere to hide.

'Would you like some advice, young lady?' asked the librarian kindly from his desk, gazing at her over his spectacles. He was small but not in the least dangerous.

Connie looked at him blankly. Could he be an expert on murderers? 'I'd love some,' she said.

The librarian fetched a vast book from one of the glass-fronted cabinets and plonked it down in front of her. It was an encyclopedia. *Vol. 1: A to ANNOY.*

'Always good to improve the mind when one's at a loose end,' said the librarian. 'Back to school soon, eh? Go on, impress them. I've always loved encyclopedias myself.'

'You'd get on very well with my governess, Miss Poots,' said Connie. What a pity they were separated by so much water!

She flipped open a page to please him and found herself staring at *Albatross, the*.

Then her whirling thoughts found their way back to their true path.

So Hiram Fink was the culprit.

In her head Connie wrote a note under his name:

Motive (NB changed from first entry): REVENGE (blames Mr B for Mrs B's death)

He and Mr Bamberger had identical photographs of Mr Bamberger's wife. But clearly Mr Fink had cared for her too, if he still kept a photograph of her by his bedside. He had been in love with her but Mr Bamberger had married her, and when she died, Hiram Fink had blamed Mr Bamberger bitterly for her death. But he had always kept his feelings to himself and on the surface had remained Mr Bamberger's friend.

Now he could bear it no longer. This voyage on the *Princess May* was his chance. He wanted to discredit Mr Bamberger, destroy the reputation of his beautiful new ship and – and murder Mr Bamberger!

What should she do?

There was only one answer. She must tell Mr Bamberger about the gun, even though he would suffer great pain to know that his dear friend wanted to kill him.

Connie clapped the encyclopedia shut in a cloud of dust and returned it to the librarian.

'Thank you,' she said. 'I'll come back for the next volume, but now I've got something rather important to do.'

She went to Mr Bamberger's stateroom past the stewards' and bellboys' rooms, to avoid passing Hiram Fink's door. Mr Bamberger's was shut. For a moment she hesitated but not for long. She put out her hand to knock.

'What are you doing, miss?' said a voice behind her.

Connie jumped. It was a steward. She thought she recognised him from the night before; he was the one who had told Bobby not to mess about with the utility room.

'I need to speak to Mr Bamberger,' she said in a small voice, which she tried to make bigger.

'No one speaks to Mr Bamberger until after he has

finished his breakfast,' said the steward firmly, 'least of all children bothering him.'

'But he likes children,' protested Connie. 'Very much.'

'Not when he's eating his eggs sunnyside up with hash browns, he doesn't,' said the steward. 'Now run along, miss.'

Connie ran along, back the way she had come. She hung about by the lift until she thought it might be safe to try again. The passage still appeared empty. She tiptoed past the stewards' room and ran to Mr Bamberger's door.

'Come in,' said his voice, which didn't sound as if it was in the middle of eating eggs and hash browns, whatever they were; they sounded disgusting.

Connie went in. Mr Bamberger was sitting in his dining area as he had been the night before, only this time, fortunately, he was alone and there was all the untidiness of a finished breakfast before him rather than a non-existent dinner.

He looked surprised to see her and not altogether welcoming.

'Connie! This is early for a visit! I thought it was the steward. I'm afraid I've some very boring work to do, so we can't talk long.'

Connie sat down at the table and folded her arms to give her courage. 'I only want to say one thing, Mr Bamberger.'

'Would you like some coffee while you say it?' He gestured at an immense silver coffee jug and refilled his cup. 'I always have to drink coffee before I say anything at all in the morning.'

'I think I'll be all right without it,' said Connie cautiously. 'I'm not allowed to drink coffee yet, you see.'

'How wise.' He took a hearty gulp from his cup. 'So what is this one thing you want to say to me?'

She took a deep breath. 'Mr Bamberger, I'm afraid your friend Mr Fink is going to murder you!'

Mr Bamberger choked on his coffee and began coughing. His face turned red and his eyes bulged. Connie watched him in alarm and then jumped up and thumped him vigorously on the back.

He raised a weak hand and stuttered, 'Thank you, Connie, thank you. I think I may recover without your help.'

He put his coffee cup down and stared at her. 'Now, how on this sweet earth have you gotten such a crazy thought into your head?'

'Quite easily, in fact,' said Connie. 'The thing is,

I know that he loved your wife as much as you did. All these years he's been keeping it a secret! And he's come on this voyage to have his revenge at last. He's hidden a gun in his desk in order to kill you!'

Mr Bamberger leaned his head on his hands. For a moment he seemed speechless. Connie watched him anxiously. Of course it would be rather a shock: she had expected that.

At last he appeared to recover. She opened her mouth to talk further but he held up a hand. 'Connie, stop right there! I have some questions for you and they're very important. How do you know that he loved my wife?' He looked across at his own photograph as he spoke and for an instant an expression of pain crossed his face.

Connie hesitated. She knew she was wading in unfamiliar grown-up waters and for a moment she wasn't absolutely sure how to tell him the dreadful truth.

'I'm afraid – I'm most awfully sorry to tell you – Mr Fink has the same photograph of your wife by his bedside.'

Mr Bamberger frowned. 'He showed it to you?'

'Not exactly,' admitted Connie. 'I – er – saw it. He wasn't there.'

'And so you concluded that he must have loved my wife?'

Connie nodded. There was something in Mr Bamberger's expression that was making this all surprisingly difficult.

'And what about the gun? You happened to see this too, when Mr Fink wasn't there?'

Connie nodded again. 'I found it, sort of by accident.'

'And was it sort of by accident that you were in Mr Fink's stateroom in the first place?'

That seemed the least important question to ask, thought Connie. But in the interests of science, anthropologists must always search for the truth and tell it when they found it. So it was important to answer questions truthfully even if they seemed the wrong ones. And Mr Bamberger had sounded disconcertingly severe.

'I thought Mr Fink might well be behind everything that's been going on,' she blurted out. 'I went into his stateroom while he was still at breakfast to find evidence. That's when I saw the photograph and found the gun.'

'I see,' said Mr Bamberger heavily. He thought for a moment while Connie brimmed with impatience.

He should call the security men and order them to restrain Mr Fink!

'Connie,' said Mr Bamberger and his voice was grave. 'I know that you wish to protect me and that's real sweet. But I must tell you that you have it all wrong here. Hiram Fink and I were never rivals in love. I told you we grew up together, boys next door. My beloved wife was Hiram's sister. He was very close to her. We were both devastated when she died.' He cleared his throat. 'I don't think either of us have ever truly recovered.'

Connie looked down at the toast crumbs on the tablecloth.

'I'm so sorry,' she whispered. What a mistake to have made! And now she had made Mr Bamberger think sadly about his dead wife for a reason that didn't exist.

She thought about Hiram Fink wanting to buy the Shining Seas shipping line, but didn't dare mention it. 'What about the gun?' she said at last. 'Why should he have a gun with him?'

'I guess I didn't know that he had one on board, but you know something? Hiram's an extremely wealthy man, a genius at making money. Several attempts to kidnap Hiram have been made in the States. He's an extremely wealthy man, a genius at making money. He goes in fear of it happening again. He would be forced to tell them which bank stores his funds and sign a letter authorising them to take it out. I daresay he always travels with a pistol these days. It's for protection, Connie, not assassination! Hiram would never hurt a hair of my head. He's always been like an older brother to me.'

'Oh,' said Connie, mortified. She felt tears prick behind her eyelids. How could a budding anthropologist have got it all so horribly wrong? She had not been at all scientific and had allowed her imagination to take over. Now dear Mr Bamberger would be cross with her. He would never want to take tea with her again!

At last she raised her eyes to his. She saw to her relief that he was smiling at her, a strange twisted smile, but it was still a smile. Then he put his warm, plump hand on hers.

'Connie,' he said gently. 'Remember that not everything is as it appears. It's a real useful lesson for life.' He smiled properly. 'And certainly for an anthropologist!'

Connie nodded, a lump in her throat. How complex humans were! She had so much to learn.

'And Connie,' said Mr Bamberger, as she went to the door. 'Don't go investigating any more of my guests, OK? I am quite safe, I do assure you.'

Connie had her back to him as she went out. He didn't see her sudden frown.

17

Connie felt restless and unhappy. She knew Miss Poots would say to her, 'What you need my girl is a breath of fresh air to blow the cobwebs away!' and she wanted to blow the cobwebs of the morning as far away as possible.

She wandered on to the promenade deck and was suddenly aware that the weather had worsened. A grey mid-morning had turned into a greyer late-morning and a fine mist of rain was darkening the decks.

It was particularly wetting rain, so Connie, dressed only in her pinafore and day dress, thought she would go and stand beneath the awning at the stern. The ship was no longer gliding smoothly through the waves as it had done earlier but beginning to roll a little in a rising wind that lifted her hair and blew on her hot cheeks as she hurried along the deck.

She passed the steamy windows of the first-class lounge as she went, and saw passengers inside playing bridge, as stewards wove around them balancing trays of coffee. She glimpsed Mrs Cartmell studying her cards with a satisfied smile. She was playing with Biffer Smith, his face truculent as always, and Door and Veer, who were winking at each other in a conspiratorial way. She saw Hiram Fink sitting alone, as he always did. She also saw Louie Leblank flitting between the tables with his stuck-on smile. She could almost hear him say, 'Everything OK, guys?'

There was a lot you could see from the outside, looking in, while you slipped by unnoticed. For an anthropologist, it was a useful and rather jolly study. Connie cheered up a little.

It was decidedly damp and becoming damper as she reached the shelter of the awning.

There were two people there already: one was Elmer, the other, well wrapped up in her coat and hat, was Mrs Pope.

'Connie, my dear,' said Muriel Pope. 'Don't catch a chill out here in that thin frock!'

Elmer raised a hand in greeting. He looked distinctly relieved not to have Mrs Pope all to himself any more. 'Hi, Connie.'

Connie's heart sank. She had wanted to be on her own to think and to watch the wash streaming out behind the ship. It was her favourite pastime on the *Princess May*, apart from eating.

'Hello,' she said politely. 'Don't you play bridge, Mrs Pope? I saw Mrs Cartmell in the lounge.'

But Mrs Pope showed no sign of resigning her tight hold on the deck rail.

'Mrs Pope doesn't play bridge, Connie,' said Elmer. He looked at Connie a little desperately.

'Oh, dear,' said Connie. 'But it's cold out here, isn't it? Wouldn't you prefer to sit in the lounge where it's warm, Mrs Pope?'

'Oh, no, my dear,' said Mrs Pope. Her voice trembled – or perhaps she was merely shivering with cold; Connie was shivering herself, in spite of the shelter of the awning. Overhead the sky had darkened ominously, so it might almost have been late evening. 'I'm keeping my eyes open for that bird again. I was telling Elmer all about it.'

'What bird, Mrs Pope?' said Connie. She noticed that Muriel Pope looked pale and rather wild altogether today, her hair blown in wisps under her hat and her ill-fitting coat bundled about her, its buttons done up wrongly.

186

'I don't want to frighten you, Connie.'

Behind Mrs Pope's back Elmer winked at Connie. 'Nothing frightens Connie,' he said eagerly. 'She's our onboard detective!'

Mrs Pope looked taken aback. 'Detective?'

'Not really a detective,' said Connie. 'But I'm interested in people. I want to be an anthropologist when I grow up, you see.'

'Yeah, she's been watching everyone to find out who's behind all the bad things that have happened. She'll find out who spilled all the oil and who pushed my marm.'

'And have you found out who yet, dear?' Muriel Pope looked nervously about her as if the someone might be creeping up on them.

'No, but I mean to,' said Connie. 'I'm trying to find evidence.' She frowned at Elmer. She didn't want him to say any more. It was embarrassing: grown-ups always thought that kind of thing was a game.

'Something has frightened you, though, hasn't it, Mrs Pope?' she went on quickly, before Mrs Pope could ask more. 'A bird, you said.'

Muriel Pope clutched the deck rail tighter as the ship gave a stronger roll. 'It was just before Elmer joined me,' she said in a quavering voice. 'I was walking along the deck when I saw it overhead, very white against the storm clouds. A huge bird!'

'Strange to see a bird out here in the mid-Atlantic,' said Connie. 'Why did it frighten you?'

'I rather think it was an albatross! You know, the bird of doom! And this voyage has been doomed, hasn't it? Right from the very start!'

And to Connie and Elmer's astonishment she began declaiming some lines of poetry in unexpectedly ringing tones.

> *'And some in dreams assurèd were*
> *Of the spirit that plagued us so;*
> *Nine fathom deep he had followed us*
> *From the land of mist and snow.'*

Connie recognised them: they were from Coleridge's *The Rime of the Ancient Mariner*. Miss Poots, her governess, had recited the poem to her with equal relish, if less drama.

Mrs Pope turned to Connie and Elmer. 'The albatross is the soul of a drowned sailor! That poor boy, you know! Something dreadful must take place, I know it!'

Connie put a hand on her coat sleeve. 'It's all right, Mrs Pope. I don't think you get albatrosses in the Atlantic.'

Mrs Pope turned and gazed at her, puzzled. 'Don't you?' She seemed almost disappointed. 'Perhaps it was something else I saw.'

'Clouds can look a bit like birds,' put in Elmer helpfully.

'Yes, perhaps it was a cloud.' Mrs Pope sounded doubtful and a touch resentful.

'Anyway, it's only bad luck if you shoot them, like in the poem' said Connie.

Mrs Pope nodded. 'We shall just have to cope with the storm as best we can. I hope this ship has enough lifeboats! I'm afraid we are in for some bad weather. Look at the colour of the sea!'

It was a bitter dark grey, against which the tops of the waves were curdled yellow, pitted with the rain which had now stared to fall heavily. It drummed on the canvas awning overhead.

'I'm going to retreat inside, children,' said Mrs Pope. 'We'll be soaked through, standing here. Elmer, your mama won't be pleased if you ruin that coat!'

For a moment Elmer's face had its old frightened look at the mention of his mother. Then he lifted his chin. 'Guess so, but I'll come in when I feel like it, Mrs Pope.'

As Mrs Pope hurried away, he turned to Connie. 'I wanted to say thanks for your help last night. You'll find out who pushed Marmee, won't you?'

'I'm not sure,' said Connie. 'I don't seem to have been very clever so far.'

'You are the cleverest person I know, Connie,' said Elmer solemnly. 'How come you know that you don't find albatrosses in the Atlantic?'

'Only in the Southern Ocean and the North Pacific,' Connie said, with an authoritative nod.

Elmer whistled. 'Lolla palooza! See what I mean?'

They entered the warm, tobacco-scented lounge and Connie's heart sank.

She could see the bedraggled, windswept figure of Muriel Pope, still in her wet coat, standing by Mrs Cartmell's bridge table and gesticulating at the window. Four faces looked up at her: sceptical (Mrs Cartmell), fascinated (Biffer Smith), nervous (Door and Veer).

Then as one they stared out. Door and Veer even left the table and teetered over to get a better view, clutching each other for balance. Biffer had already taken out his notebook and was starting to scribble; there was nothing Connie could do about it.

'I'll see you at lunch,' she said to Elmer.

'Don't you want to come and play billiards?' he said, disappointed. He hadn't started to look green yet.

'I'd love to another time. But there's something I must do.'

Hiram Fink cut a lonely figure sitting by himself, his greying hair combed neatly over his large forehead. Connie went and stood by him in her damp dress and pinafore until he looked up from his papers in surprise.

'I rather think I might like to learn about stocks and shares, after all,' she said gently. 'That is, if you'd still like to teach me, Mr Fink.'

It was time for luncheon. A steward had gone through the first-class lounge, banging a gong.

Connie's head was reeling from explanations and her eyes were blurred by figures but Hiram Fink had enjoyed the last couple of hours enormously.

'I suppose you still want to be an anthropologist?' he said. 'You might make an admirable stockbroker.

We need women in the profession.'

'You're a very good teacher, Mr Fink. I think I'm better suited to anthropology but I've learned such a lot. My governess, Miss Poots, will be so impressed. She's very enthusiastic about new opportunities for women.' Connie's tummy rumbled. 'Shall we go down to luncheon?' she added hopefully.

'Of course, my dear. Let me escort you.'

They looked around. Somehow, while Hiram Fink had been talking, the lounge had gradually emptied without either of them noticing. There were one or two card tables still occupied, people gallantly playing on while the ship rocked beneath them, but otherwise they were almost alone.

'Goodness,' said Mr Fink in astonishment, clutching the table for balance as he rose to his feet. 'People must be hungry today!'

But the special guests' table was almost empty too, as they discovered when at length they had managed to negotiate the stairs down to the first-class dining saloon. Connie wasn't certain whether Hiram's Fink's courteous arm was helping her, or if it was the other way around.

Only Cornelia Cartmell sat at their table, holding forth between mouthfuls to a queasy-looking Muriel

Pope, who had scarcely touched her food. On the other hand, Mrs Cartmell looked as if she was going to devour the full six courses.

All around the table, where clever little twiddly walls had been flipped up to prevent plates flying off, were half-finished servings of food that the stewards hadn't yet cleared away. It seemed as if the other guests had risen as one and rushed out of the dining saloon, perhaps driven by a particularly determined heave beneath the ship.

After a couple of courses, Connie excused herself to Mr Fink – 'I should go and see how my cousin is' – and lurched across to the door. A bellboy held it open for her.

'Bobby!' she whispered. 'I must talk to you!'

He followed her out into the shifting passage; he was without his skates because of the weather. 'What's up, mate?' He looked at her warily. 'I shouldn't be talking to you. Can't risk getting into Mr B's bad books!'

Connie balanced herself against the wall; the passages had helpful rails either side for heavy seas.

'I want you to know that I don't suspect you!'

'Decent of you,' he said gloomily. 'Does that mean you've found out who's behind it all?'

'Not yet.'

Bobby came closer. 'There is something,' he whispered. 'It could be a clue.'

'What?'

'The utility room wasn't locked while her ladyship was in there yesterday evening! I didn't say nothing at the time – it just pretended to unlock it – but she could have got out any time, all by herself! I call that a rum do.'

Connie stared at him for a moment. Then she seized his arm and nearly fell over as the passage tilted beneath her. 'Then that means, Bobby, she's our main suspect!'

'Does it?'

'Yes, don't you see? She must have been just fibbing! Telling everybody that she'd been pushed in was utter rot. There was no tall, strong figure in yellow overalls at all!'

'But why should she do that?'

'To divert suspicion from herself.'

'But someone almost pushed her overboard this afternoon!'

'She must have made that up too, Bobby. She must be behind all the other things as well!'

'But why?'

Connie clung on to the rail passage as the ship gave a juddering leap.

'I think she's doing it for her husband. They're living apart, but perhaps he's asked her to do this for him and it's a way for her to regain his affection. There are lots of romantic novels in her stateroom. I think she yearns to be back with him.'

He stared at her, open-mouthed.

'I need to go into her room again to search for incriminating evidence. You've got to help me, Bobby! I want you to unlock the door for me!'

'Not sure about this, Connie, not sure at all. We'll be nabbed!'

'Not if we're careful,' she said impatiently. 'Please, Bobby. Mr Bamberger will thank us, you'll see. You don't want any more beastly things to happen, do you? Poor Mr Bamberger. If the ship's reputation is damaged, he will be too!'

'All right,' he said reluctantly. 'I'll open the door for you but then I'm off, mate.'

'Thank you! You're an utter brick!'

'I'll say this for you, Connie Carew, you're a plucky little thing and no mistake. When shall we do it?'

'Now! While she's in the salon. Come on!'

18

Connie was disappointed in Bobby. True to his word, he had shot off immediately once he had opened the door of Mrs Cartmell's stateroom. A more gallant gentleman, like Arthur, say, would have lingered longer, ready to defend her while she was inside. But Arthur, sadly, had other things on his mind now, like Ida.

Connie wasn't sure how long Mrs Cartmell would manage to carry on eating until she, too, succumbed to seasickness like everyone else. She knew she had very limited time.

The pile of romantic novels were still by the bedside, the top one with a silk bookmark sticking out and a pair of spectacles on top. Elmer smiled at her from the photograph frame, making her feel like a traitor.

The stateroom had been tidied by the bedroom steward that morning, so there were no clothes lying about; she would have to go through Mrs Cartmell's drawers and investigate the cupboard and linen lockers. That made Connie feel distinctly awkward, but she persevered: somewhere she would find some evidence, she was absolutely certain.

Goodness, what a lot of clothes Mrs Cartmell owned!

On the dressing-table there were only a pair of blue-backed hairbrushes and a clothes-brush, a very small bottle of eau de Cologne and a box of face-powder. No rouge pot or lip colour. Clearly Mrs Cartmell did not believe in making a silly fuss about her face.

There was no sign of anything that could be called 'evidence' anywhere: Connie even patted the satin linings of Mrs Cartmell's calf suitcases to make sure there was nothing hidden in them.

Muriel Pope had the much smaller maid's room off Mrs Cartmell's and there was a shared bathroom in the tiny passageway. Connie put her nose round the bathroom door and did a quick survey. Ordinary bathroom things: face-flannels, a bar of Pears soap, two tins of tooth powder tactfully placed some way apart by the steward so the owners would not get them mixed.

Connie was just withdrawing her head from the bathroom when she heard to her horror a fumbling at the door of Mrs Cartmell's stateroom. Heavy footsteps lurched into the room and then there was a mutter.

'I'm sure I locked that door before luncheon!'

Then Mrs Cartmell's key was turned firmly in the lock – on the inside.

For a moment Connie froze. Botheration! If Mrs Cartmell came to the bathroom, all would be up. She would be discovered.

As she clutched the corner of the bathroom door, the ship gave a tremendous roll and Connie was flung sideways into Muriel Pope's cabin. In a flash she was under the bed, scarcely breathing, the carpet soft and new and very clean beneath her and the stout leg of the bedside table almost touching her face.

Next door she could hear groans as Mrs Cartmell, too, was thrown off course and subsided on to her protesting bed.

How on earth was she going to get out, thought Connie, now that she was locked in with Mrs Cartmell? The only way she could escape was through Muriel Pope's door but it was locked, too. Otherwise she would have to wait until Mrs Cartmell pressed her bell for a bellboy – and it might not be Bobby

– and she would have to slip out then somehow.

All she could do now was wait and see what happened and try to prepare her apologies.

Next door Mrs Cartmell's luncheon of several courses had its effect and despite the pitching of the ship she began to snore loudly.

Connie lay spread-eagled, her chin on the carpet and her fingers digging deep into the pile. It was the only way she could remain under Muriel Pope's bed without being rolled out. Above and around her she could hear objects shifting about above the rumble of Mrs Cartmell's snores.

The furniture on the *Princess May* was fastened down in case of heavy weather, but something was sliding about on the bedside table above her, scraping on the wood. Then whatever it was fell off and almost hit Connie's nose. She squinted at it and put up her hand to examine it better. A small round pill-box.

Connie read the label. They were Muriel Pope's sleeping pills. *Two to be taken at bedtime.* **Warning:** *Do not exceed the recommended dose.*

Something heavier came down next and landed with a thud near her hand. A leather-bound copy of the Bible. So she had something to read, even though a Bible might not have been her first choice. She opened it and stared at the writing on the end-papers.

To Wilfred on his Confirmation

There was a crash as a tin of Huntley and Palmers digestive biscuits fell off the dressing-table, scattering the biscuits in all directions. Several were easily within Connie's reach. At least she wouldn't starve.

Next door Mrs Cartmell snored on.

With a soft woosh a couple of Mrs Pope's dingy hats fell down from the top of the wardrobe and landed on the carpet a few feet away. Then there was a veritable shower of objects from the bedside table: some of them skidded and landed on top of the bed, others fell near Connie. Mrs Pope's travelling clock landed with a twang next to her elbow, her spectacle case made a graceful dive; a metal nail-file and cuticle stick swooped down together.

Something was stuck in the back end-paper of the Bible, like a treasured souvenir that might have been used once as a marker and then forgotten about. Connie had to peer at it sideways to see it properly.

It was a dog-eared theatre programme. As far as reading material was concerned, it was much jollier entertainment than the Bible and very much shorter. It was dated some fifteen years earlier, the programme for an end of the pier show that Mrs Pope must have enjoyed, perhaps with her husband before he ran off, thought Connie.

Madcap Midsummer! Starring Miss Maisie Mason and Miss Olive Harbottle.

There was a blurred photograph of the two girls with their arms around each other, wearing baggy bathing-dresses and sitting on the steps of a bathing-machine. They didn't look as glamorous as Door and Veer but perhaps it was just a bad photograph. After all, it was so long ago.

It was most amusing, Connie thought, to read about something that had taken place before she was born!

She had read it from cover to cover when she heard the key turn in the lock of the door and Mrs Pope staggered in.

19

Connie saw her feet in their sensible shoes weave from side to side as she tried to avoid treading on her hats and keep her balance. She crunched across the broken digestive biscuits and managed to reach the bathroom, where Connie heard her being rather ill.

Throughout all this Mrs Cartmell's snores continued, with a particularly loud snort at one crucial moment of poor Mrs Pope's distress.

Connie didn't waste time.

Now was her chance to escape, while Mrs Pope was still in the bathroom. She heard the splash of water and a muffled groan. By this time she had wriggled out from under the bed and was struggling to get to the door across the wildly rocking room, hanging on to the backs of chairs and the edge of the dressing-table.

She was at the door when Mrs Pope staggered out of the bathroom. There was a terrible pause while she stared at Connie, her face very white and her hair hanging down in straggles.

Connie, startled, tried to pull herself together. She knew that she looked a mess herself, her sailor dress much crumpled from her time under the bed.

They both spoke at once, while Mrs Cartmell slept on noisily next door.

'Gracious, child, whatever are you doing in my cabin? I . . .'

'Oh, bother, I must be in the wrong one. I'm so sorry, Mrs Pope. I . . .'

'. . . haven't been at all well.'

'. . . am such a duffer,' Connie went on, her hand on the door handle. 'I lost my balance, I mean my bearings. I do apologise . . .'

'Could you please go?' Mrs Pope finished weakly, sitting on her bed. In her distress she didn't seem to notice the lameness of Connie's excuse. 'I should like to lie down.'

'Of course,' Connie said in relief, her hand already on the door handle.

Outside, she clutched the passage rail and began to work her way along to her own stateroom. Her heart was beating hard. Ahead of her she could see Bobby walking towards her with an easy sailor's gait, his legs spread apart for balance and a grin on his face. He looked remarkably chipper, she thought sourly.

'Did you get nabbed?'

'Yes, I did! I had a beastly time in there! I was locked in on both sides. Why didn't you come and rescue me?'

'What? Face that old dragon? Not blooming likely.'

'You could have brought her a cup of tea or something – pretended you thought she'd ordered it. Then you could have left the door unlocked for me. I call it a pretty poor show, Bobby!'

'But I'm not like you, mate.' He looked at her admiringly. 'You think of everything. I could never have worked that one out for myself.'

Connie was a little appeased. It was difficult to remain in a wax with Bobby for long.

'Did you find any evidence?'

She shook her head. 'Nothing at all.'

Bobby left her at her stateroom and went whistling on, past the closed doors. Connie unlocked her door and paused. A scrap of white paper lay on the polished floor outside. It must have dropped out of Bobby's pocket, or perhaps he had been holding it in his hand while he helped her along.

Managing not to fall flat on her face, she bent and picked it up. Something was scribbled on it in pencil. A message for Bobby. She called out after him.

When he had swayed back up to her with that easy sailor's motion she held it out to him. 'You dropped this.'

He took it from her and blushed to the roots of his hair. 'Thanks,' he muttered. He looked extraordinarily guilty.

Connie stared after him, puzzled. She had, of course, managed to read what was on the paper. It was very short. *Meet 2300*

How very curious – and how intriguing.

Ida was lying on her bed, groaning.

Connie lowered herself carefully into the armchair, which seemed to be steady enough until the ship rolled again, when it was a little like a small ship itself. Clutching the arms, she thought hard. What was the significance of those numbers? Who or what was 2300?

Then she realised. It was the time on a ship's twenty-four-hour clock. Sailors counted the hours from midnight. So 2300 would be eleven o'clock at night. Bobby was going to meet someone then.

Surely Bobby couldn't be a suspect after all? Was he in league with someone? She didn't want to believe it but she would have to make sure.

'Ida?' she began.

There was another groan from the bed. Ida raised herself on her elbows.

'Oh, Connie, I confess I'm fearfully frightened. Is the ship going to sink, do you think? Shall I call Arthur? He's lying next door but we should be together at the end.'

'I don't think there's anything to be worried about,' said Connie briskly. 'Anyway, there are enough lifeboats to go round.'

Ida didn't sound much reassured by this information. She gave a wail as the ship lurched.

'I need to ask you some questions,' said Connie.

Another groan, incredulous this time. 'Wha-at?'

'It will take your mind off being sick, you'll see. First of all, how well do you know Bobby Sparrow?'

'Orphan Bobby from the Sisters of Hope?'

'Yes, Bobby Sparrow,' said Connie impatiently.

'He didn't have a surname, really,' moaned Ida.

'Then why was he called Sparrow?'

'He was like a sparrow, that's why, a cheeky little chap.'

Ida moaned as the ship rolled. 'Oh, I don't 'alf feel awful, Connie – half, I mean.'

'Was he mischievous? I mean, did he enjoy playing pranks?'

'Oh, yes! I remember once he put a dead rat in Mrs Goodenough's bed. That was a laugh, that was!'

'But would you say there was any malice behind his pranks?'

'Not Bobby. It was larks with him. He's a decent little fellow.' Ida propped herself up on her elbows and stared at Connie. 'Something's up, isn't it?' Her eyes lit with excitement and she forgot to groan as the boat rolled again. 'I say, Connie, is he sweet on you? I'm not sure Mother would approve!'

'Mother' was Connie's Aunt Dorothea, and Ida was still getting used to the word, so she hesitated over it. She smiled teasingly. 'You and an orphan bellboy, Connie! I never!'

'Don't be a duffer,' said Connie crossly. 'Besides, you were an orphan, too, not long ago! If you really want to know, I'm carrying out an investigation into the mishaps on the *Princess May*.'

'Good for you,' said Ida. She lowered herself gloomily back on to her pillows. 'It will be the biggest mishap of all if the *Princess May* sinks!'

But the ship didn't sink. During the rest of the afternoon and evening the rolling grew gentler until it became quite bearable, even for those who had been most indisposed.

Dinner was delayed until the guests had recovered their usual appetites, and by the time a bellboy sounded the gong through the first-class passages there was an unseemly stampede down to the dining saloon.

Connie sat next to Arthur at the special guests' table. When she asked him the time at various intervals between courses, he patiently complied, pulling out his pocket watch to check, as he rushed back from piano-playing. At last he grew puzzled and somewhat suspicious. 'I say, Connie, what's up, old thing?'

'I read somewhere that young ladies should have plenty of beauty sleep,' said Connie, with a yawn. 'And what with chaperoning you two in the evening, I don't think I've been getting enough. It's doing nothing for my looks.'

Arthur considered her. 'You look healthy enough to me.'

'Health is not the same as beauty, Arthur.' Connie yawned again, hugely. 'And I am a little tired.'

He was immediately contrite. 'Dear Connie. You've been looking after us so splendidly. You've been an absolute brick! Of course you must go to bed.'

'Not yet,' said Connie, alarmed. 'I haven't had my pudding! But perhaps you could tell me when it's a quarter to eleven?'

'That's very precise,' said Arthur, still a little puzzled. 'But of course I will.'

So at a quarter to eleven Connie left the guests eating savouries and made her way back up to the first-class passages. In her stateroom she changed out of her dinner slippers and into her soft deck shoes. She was going to have to be as quiet as possible if she was to follow Bobby unnoticed.

Many of the stewards and bellboys were still on the decks below, but she hadn't seen Bobby among them. She loitered in the bend at the top of the passage so that she could watch the bellboys' room. She had not been there long when the door opened and out sloped Bobby. He wasn't wearing his roller-skates.

Fortunately for Connie, he turned right, away from where she stood. He passed the lift, crossed the landing and took the passage opposite their own. Connie followed him like a shadow, hoping he wouldn't turn round.

People passed, returning from dinner, passengers who didn't want to dance or indulge in the evening's entertainment, and she hid behind them. No one paid any attention to a girl in a knee-length muslin dress; she might have been invisible.

Bobby had reached the end: he could go no further. Connie, some way behind, saw him disappear behind a door she had not noticed before. When she came up to it she saw it had a notice: **Service Only.**

Quietly she opened it and slipped inside.

She was standing at the head of a long flight of narrow, uncarpeted stairs that led down and down. Somewhere, a flight below her perhaps, she could hear Bobby's feet in their smart black shoes clipping the steps. He was moving fast.

She began to descend, clinging to the iron rail that was all that prevented her from falling down the deep dark well of the staircase; it was not well lit.

She must have passed several floors or 'decks' by now, narrow landings with doors off them. She was feeling dizzy with the speed but she didn't want to lose Bobby.

At last she looked down and saw she was on the very last flight. Bobby, at the bottom, opened a door, and as he did so a blast of hot, steamy air gushed out, smelling acrid and strange – of earth and the charcoal pencils that Connie used in her drawing lessons. There was a strange, frightening noise, too – the great, endless pounding of heavy and metallic masses being shunted to and fro somewhere; and a red glowing light that flickered up the staircase, almost to where she stood.

Then the door had closed behind him and he had vanished.

Her heart thudding, Connie stepped cautiously off the bottom step and went a pace or two forward to the door. A notice on it read: **DANGER! NO UNAUTHORISED PERSONNEL** in large red capitals.

Connie knew that 'unauthorised personnel' meant her and for a moment she faltered. But she couldn't give up now.

She put her hand on the door, which vibrated strangely under her fingers and was warm to the touch.

It didn't have a handle but an odd metal device which she had to work out before she could open it. It took her some moments – precious moments in which she knew Bobby would be getting away from her – but she managed it in the end.

She had never come across such a heavy door in her life. She pushed with all her might and eventually it gave and she stepped through.

20

She was standing at the end of a tunnel but it might have been the entrance to Hell.

Black, nightmare figures moved jerkily in the distance, shouting and gesticulating, pushing darker objects in front of them. Were they human? Some of them looked as if they had five limbs or grossly mishapen backs. She could make nothing out clearly, such was the all-enveloping fug of steam.

There were rooms off the tunnel – doorless rooms. Who could live in such a fearful place?

All the same, figures were disappearing inside. A tremendous crash would follow and the heat would intensify until it became almost unbearable. The noise reminded Connie of coals cascading into the coal hole of her London house. But this crash was magnified a million times, as if from a vast avalanche. Then a stream of sparks shot out through the opening to the room until, after a deafening clang that reverberated right around the tunnel, they were drawn back in and swallowed somehow, leaving behind air that was hotter and thicker than ever.

For a moment Connie's courage deserted her. She had never been anywhere as dreadful.

She crouched back miserably against the wall of the tunnel, her ears ringing. She put her hands up to shield them and saw that somehow her fingers had become covered in filth. Sweat was streaming off her. She wondered if her hair was on fire. Her face felt burning and her best dinner dress was covered in smuts.

Then someone or something loomed over her. A black, glistening face looked down on her and a hole opened in it. Teeth gleamed as a voice said, gruffly, 'Hey, what have we here?'

Connie couldn't speak for a moment. Her brain was stultified by heat. She fell back lamely on her old excuse. 'I'm sorry. I've lost my way.' It came out as a scorched whisper.

'Well, you won't find it here, little lass!'

Then Connie saw Bobby come up behind the man. He was brushing himself down and evidently about to leave: Bobby, in his red jacket and pill-box hat, looking as out of place as she felt in her no-longer white dress.

His mouth dropped open when he saw her. He looked mortified and furious but also alarmed. He turned quickly to the man. 'It's all right, Mister Stoker. She's from my deck. I'll take her back up.'

'Friend of yours, is she?' the stoker grunted. He gave Bobby a wink, then turned and left them.

'Come on!' hissed Bobby. He almost dragged Connie to the door in the tunnel that led to the stairs. 'What are you doing down here?'

Connie's legs were trembling but she recovered sufficiently to retort, 'What are *you* doing here?'

He didn't answer her question. His eyes narrowed. 'Did you follow me? It's no place for the likes of you. Do you know what this place is?'

'It's where people make the ship work. I don't know how, though.'

'Don't understand how it works myself. But it's dangerous, mate. There are great machines and boilers of burning steam and furnaces full of fire, and Lord knows what. You shouldn't have come. You could get me into trouble.'

'I'm sorry, Bobby,' said Connie meekly. She could see he was upset. Was that because he was anxious on her behalf, or because he was put out at being followed to a secret meeting place?

'Lucky I know that stoker,' said Bobby. 'He's a decent fellow and won't tell on me.'

They went up one flight of stairs and then Bobby led her out to find the lift. Connie was glad because her legs felt too shaky to climb right up to the first-class deck.

They didn't speak to each other as the lift went up. Bobby didn't meet her eye. Who had he met down there? As other passengers entered at each deck she was unable to ask him any questions.

Perfumed ladies in long silk skirts and gentlemen in white ties looked curiously at her, at her dirty hands and even dirtier dress, still damp from steam. They raised their eyebrows at one another, wrinkling their noses and edging away.

'Gracious, Gerald, look at that child! Whatever are her parents thinking of? Letting her roam all over the ship at this hour!'

'Probably comes from steerage class. Look at the state of her!'

When Connie looked indignantly at the long lift mirror to check, she saw to her dismay that the back of her dress was smeared black from crouching against the wall of the tunnel. A good deal seemed to have spread to her face and hands, too, and she probably smelled of smoke and engine grease. But anthropologists on the trail of new discoveries must get quite as dirty exploring different places, just as she had been!

Yet somehow, irritatingly, Bobby looked as smart as he had when he first left the promenade deck, the brass buttons on his red jacket shining brightly and his black trousers still in their knife-edged creases. He leaped in and out of the lift, opening and shutting the gates for the passengers. People thanked him and he smiled winningly each time and wished them a polite goodnight.

As soon as they reached the bridge deck he was caught by a steward. 'Ah, there you are, my lad! Last job of the evening for you. Number 24's bell's just gone. Off you go.'

As Bobby shot off, the steward glanced at Connie's clothes but was too tactful to say anything.

Connie retreated to her stateroom. Ida had not yet returned from dancing. She undressed, bundled her dirty dress under the bed and tried to wash off the worst of the dirt on her hands and face. Then she climbed into bed and opened her notebook disconsolately.

She wrote *Bobby Sparrow: why engine rooms?* in a

half-hearted way. She refused to believe he could be behind everything when he had helped her so much.

Under *Cornelia Cartmell* she wrote *utility room unlocked! (??) No incriminating evidence found in stateroom.* Where she might have hidden a set of yellow overalls and a container of black oil Connie didn't know, and somehow she couldn't imagine the fastidious Cornelia Cartmell clambering into anything as undignified as baggy overalls.

No, she must have missed some vital clue somewhere, but she couldn't see what it could be. She sensed that all the mishaps on the *Princess May* were leading up to some terrible climax that would take place before the ship reached its destination.

Now she only had a day left in which to work out who had been causing them and if there would be any more victims.

21

The last day dawned warm and sunny. Outside the portholes the sea was calm. The ship had stopped rocking and only now and then gave a little judder, as if it were breathing out a sigh of relief.

Connie looked out for Bobby as she went down to breakfast with Ida and Arthur but he was clearly being kept busy by the steward after his absence the night before. Then the three of them decided to have a final game of deck quoits. Or at least Connie and Arthur did.

Ida lay basking in a deckchair, her face shielded from the sun by a large sailor hat, watching them lazily, her back to the sea as usual. Today there was scarcely a wind to ruffle the pages of her magazine; only warm passing air as the ship glided along. Biffer Smith sat writing up his notes a little further along, clad in a bathing-suit, striped in red and white, that came down to his chunky knees. His calves below were thick and white and covered in short black hairs. Connie stared at them, fascinated, but Ida averted her eyes primly.

'If only the weather could have been like this every day,' she murmured.

'Yes, indeed,' said a voice not far away.

Connie looked over and all she could see beyond the back of the person's deckchair were a pair of hands knitting something small and beige. Because of the colour she knew it must be Mrs Pope sitting there. The hands flicked the wool in and out deftly – smooth but workmanlike hands – and the needles clicked.

Connie had always wondered about the attraction of knitting: Miss Poots sometimes took out her knitting to pass the time when Connie was struggling with a Latin translation. It seemed both complicated and boring, but it was undoubtedly fascinating to watch. She wandered over and perched on the end of Ida's deckchair, gazing mesmerised at Mrs Pope's flashing hands.

'What are you knitting? Is it for a grandchild?' she asked politely, anxious to make up for trespassing in Mrs Pope's stateroom the day before, even though at breakfast she had apologised again and Mrs Pope had had a little laugh about it.

'A grandchild?' echoed Ida. 'Oh, how sweet!'

'What a sensible colour,' added Connie. 'It won't show the baby's sick.'

'Connie!' exclaimed Ida. She smiled apologetically at Mrs Pope.

'It isn't for a grandchild,' said Mrs Pope, gazing at them earnestly through her spectacles. 'I don't have one. It's a scarf for Missions to Seamen, the charity. I do like to support them.'

'I'm sure it will be appreciated,' said Ida gamely. She leaned over, her perfect face close to Mrs Pope's, and whispered, 'What have you done with your employer this morning?'

For a moment Mrs Pope looked startled. Everyone was always astonished by Ida's beauty, especially when they saw it close up.

'Mrs Cartmell is planning what to wear this evening. She was arguing with the Purser when I left her. She didn't want me there while she was trying on costumes.' She sighed. 'I believe she is coming up to join me soon.'

'Arthur, dear,' Ida said with relief, as he approached. 'Shall we go for a turn around the deck?'

'I'll stay here,' said Connie. 'I am feeling a little tired.'

Ida gave her a suspicious look but she was so anxious to avoid Cornelia Cartmell that she didn't linger. She took Arthur by the arm and steered him rapidly away.

Connie removed herself to a deckchair a little way from the others but still within good eavesdropping distance, and settled down to wait. She could watch as well, if she peered around the wooden back of her deckchair.

Soon she saw Radmilla Oblomov coming along the deck, dressed in her dark practice clothes and ballet shoes, her black hair gleaming in the sunlight. Even when she walked, she seemed to dance. Like a beautiful black panther, she settled gracefully into a deckchair next to Muriel Pope, the effect spoiled by her rather ugly scowl.

'Where is Arthur? How am I to dance tonight with no rehearsal? I zink he has forgotten!'

'He's gone for a little walk with his fiancée, dear,' said Mrs Pope. 'He'll be back in a tick, you wait and see.'

Radmilla pouted and frowned, arching her strong but delicate feet in their satin shoes and gazing at

222

them critically. Biffer Smith gazed at her in a silent agony of admiration. She gave him not a glance.

In a short while Mrs Cartmell sailed up with her parasol and one of her much-veiled hats. She plumped herself down next to Muriel Pope and beckoned for a steward. One came hurrying up and Mrs Cartmell ordered an iced lemonade.

'It is so very hot today, isn't it?' she said loudly. 'Almost too hot. The temperature on this voyage has never been quite right, I fear.'

'I doubt that even Mr Bamberger, or the Captain for that matter, can do anything about the weather, madam,' grunted Biffer Smith. He glanced sideways at Radmilla, as if hoping for a smile, and she nodded sternly in agreement.

Mrs Cartmell regarded his bare knees with distaste and went on to complain about the Purser. 'The only costume he had left in my size for tonight was Queen Victoria. Such a paltry collection! You'd think they'd do better for a maiden voyage.'

'I think you'll make an admirable Queen Victoria,' said Muriel Pope, appearing eager to pacify her. 'You're so very stately and – er – you have a commanding presence.'

Only Connie noticed the sudden violent gleam in

her eye, as she said it. Though it vanished in an instant, she knew then that Mrs Pope hated her employer.

'Do I? Thank you, Muriel. Perhaps I shall change my mind, then.'

'You English!' exclaimed Radmilla. 'Your queen has only been dead for nine years and you pretend to be her at a party? In my country we would zink zat an insult!'

'It is a tribute,' said Cornelia Cartmell quellingly. 'I grant you that there are few who could carry it off with the right kind of respect but I will certainly do my utmost.'

Connie listened, gazing intently out to sea, as if waiting for America to appear on the horizon. No one took any notice of her.

'And what are you planning to go as, Mrs Pope?' asked Biffer Smith. It sounded as if the question was uttered more out of curiosity than kindness.

Mrs Pope grew flustered at once. 'Oh, I don't think I am. That is, I don't believe it would be quite appropriate for a companion—'

'Good heavens, woman, this is a party!'

'No doubt you have something decent to wear, Mr Smith?' said Cornelia Cartmell, with a pointed look at Biffer's bare legs.

224

Door and Veer tripped up next, in high-waisted dresses and straw hats, arms linked. They plumped themselves down next to Biffer Smith, giggling and whispering about their costumes for the evening. Cornelia Cartmell turned her face away and gave the sea a glare that should have turned it to ice.

Louie Leblank sidled up in his striped blazer, rubbing his hands together and smiling cheerily at them all. Connie noted that he had taken off the plaster on his finger. The cut was almost invisible.

'Everything OK, folks? What a beautiful day, courtesy of the *Princess May*! You have the drinks you want? Anything I can get you, just say the word!'

He bent close to Door and Veer. 'My, don't you two look pretty today!' They fluttered their eyelashes and giggled some more.

'And where's the little man?' Leblank said to Mrs Cartmell. 'Not seasick in this weather, surely?'

'My son – if that is to whom you refer – is in the library,' said Mrs Cartmell freezingly, 'Learning about albatrosses in the encyclopedia.'

Mrs Pope gave a start. Louie Leblank's face lived up to his name. Connie thought he had probably never heard of albatrosses.

'You see, my companion –' a spiteful tone entered

Cornelia Cartmell's voice '– thought she saw one yesterday. The bird of doom, you know.'

'I didn't mean to frighten the poor boy,' stammered Mrs Pope. 'I'm sure I was mistaken.'

'My Elmer is made of strong stuff.' Mrs Cartmell looked proudly at Leblank. 'He wanted to know more.'

'Most commendable, madam,' said Louie Leblank. 'But let me assure you guys that there is no doom awaiting any of us on this ship!'

'How can you be so sure?' said Biffer Smith unexpectedly. He raised himself on one elbow and looked belligerent. 'We have had plenty of warnings, haven't we?' He glowered around. 'All of us – yes, all of us – have suffered mishaps, some more serious than others.'

A murmur of agreement went up.

'I might have broken my back!' said Radmilla Oblomov.

'I thought I was bleeding to death!' said Muriel Pope. 'And then those footsteps in the night!'

'I saw the ghost!' said Door.

Mrs Cartmell refrained from saying anything about her experiences, keeping a dignified silence.

Biffer Smith raised a hand, quelling the babble. It was a powerful-looking hand, stubby-fingered but with a wide palm that seemed at that moment to hold them all within it.

He spoke loudly and with emphasis. 'These have been only a prologue. We don't know who it will be yet or why, but I believe something is going to happen to one of us before the end of the voyage that may literally be – deadly.'

Connie wrote in her head: *Why is he so sure?* Was it suspicious? Or did it mean that Biffer Smith had turned detective and discovered clues that she, Connie, hadn't?

There was a shocked silence after his remark.

'You mean – murder?' said Veer, wide-eyed.

Biffer Smith nodded grimly. 'I do indeed, young woman.'

'Nonsense, sir!' said Cornelia Cartmell but even she looked a little taken aback.

Radmilla Oblomov twisted her hands together and looked more tragic than ever; she was a believer in Fate, Connie was sure. 'It will be me, I know! Someone vishes to stop me dancing for ever!'

Muriel Pope uttered a little cry of fright and pressed the ball of beige wool to her lips. 'Oh, dear, oh dear!'

Door and Veer stared at each other and their perfectly manicured hands stretched across the space between their deckchairs to clutch the other's.

Louie Leblank's cheery smile vanished. Without it, his waxen skin looked old and creased and the dye on his hair was visible in the sun. For a moment he looked as if he disliked them all intensely.

'I must ask you, Mr Smith, sir, as politely as possible, not to frighten Mr Bamberger's guests with your fantastical notions.' He looked around, his eyes surprisingly fierce. 'Mr Bamberger has treated you all to this maiden voyage on his wonderful new ship and you have been pampered and cosseted at his expense. Do you really believe he would let anything happen to any of you?'

Then at once his usual face was back in place.

It was interesting that Louie Leblank felt genuine loyalty to Mr Bamberger, revealed in that isolated moment. It meant, Connie thought resignedly, that she would have to cross him off her list of suspects.

'Dear ladies and gents, prepare for the most splendid party tonight and forget your worries. For there is nothing to worry about, I do assure you. Tomorrow we reach New York!'

And with that, and a smile and a bow, he had gone.

Door and Veer recovered quickly. They leaned towards each other and whispered, 'Buttons!' then burst into bubbles of laughter, eyeing each other and throwing themselves back in their chairs.

'He's a traitor, you know,' said Cornelia Cartmell loudly. 'He was working for my husband.'

'Until your husband sacked him,' Biffer Smith pointed out. 'No wonder he's faithful to Bamberger now!'

Connie stood up quietly and slipped away.

She found Elmer at a table in the library, as his mother had said, poring over *Vol. 1: A to ANNOY*.

The weather had tempted passengers on to the decks and he was alone, apart from the librarian, who was sitting discreetly behind his desk and yawning behind his hand. He looked up as Connie came in and recognised her.

'You've started quite a run on that particular volume, young lady,' he whispered and nodded in Elmer's direction. 'That young man asked for it, and also a lady earlier and then a gentleman!'

'Goodness!' said Connie. Perhaps it was Muriel Pope come to reassure herself that it was not an albatross that she had seen; perhaps it was one of the other female passengers. And a gentleman?

'Can you tell me what they looked like?' she asked.

The librarian looked surprised but she could tell that he was bored and might humour her.

'The lady I don't recall. But the gentleman – he told me he was off for a swim in the first-class pool. He wasn't dressed for it but he had a towelling bag with him.'

'Thank you,' said Connie. Biffer Smith must have wanted to check on albatrosses for his notes.

She darted over to Elmer and sat down next to him. Elmer shut the encyclopedia with a thump, so that motes of dust flew up in the sunlight streaming from the porthole.

'Like you said, Mrs Pope can't have seen an albatross. How come you know so much, Connie?'

'I don't know,' said Connie modestly. 'I may have a remarkable brain.'

'Anyhow, I'm real glad you're here.' He looked at her shyly. 'I haven't had a chance to thank you for helping rescue my marm.'

Connie was touched. 'She could have got out of that cupboard at any time, you know,' she said gently. 'It wasn't locked.' Of course she couldn't mention her suspicions about his mother to Elmer, so she added, 'I think whoever pushed her in must have been disturbed by someone approaching before they had time to lock her in.'

'I know,' said Elmer. 'But Marmee didn't know it at the time.'

'Surely she tried to get out?'

Elmer hesitated. Then he leaned across and whispered, 'Can you keep a secret?'

Connie nodded, puzzled.

'Swear, then. Swear on the most precious thing you have.'

Connie opened her mouth, then paused. She couldn't swear on Arthur, or Ida, or her two aunts, because it didn't seem right to swear on people. Anyway, who was most precious to her? They all were.

'All right. I swear on my anthropology notes.'

She didn't tell Elmer that they were in a shamefully poor state at the moment, more a list of crossings-out than anything else – apart from his own mother, that was.

Elmer leaned across the table and spoke out of the corner of his mouth.

'The truth is, she's real terrified of small spaces. She doesn't like to make a fuss in case people think she's weak. She has to look strong, you see, because she's got lots of men working for her. She gets the jitters just riding in an elevator in her hotel but she hides it. She always takes the stairs here on the ship. When she was pushed into that dark place, she was so scared, she couldn't move, she told me. She couldn't even crawl to the door. If she had, she would have known it wasn't locked.'

'I see,' said Connie slowly. She thought hard. 'Do you see what this means?'

Elmer shook his head.

'Your mother's assailant might not have been interrupted, after all. She could have been pushed in by someone who knew about her fear of small spaces. I don't think it's as secret as you think, Elmer!'

22

Connie and Ida were getting ready for the fancy dress party. Ida had dragged Connie away from tea early. She wanted plenty of time to get ready, she said, and she needed Connie on hand to help her.

In between buttoning Ida into Salacia's costume Connie sat on the sofa, staring at her oil-stained handkerchiefs. She looked at her notebook and wished it wasn't quite so full of crossings-out.

She also wished she had been able to have tea with Mr Bamberger on their very last day, but he had said sadly that he must write his speech for the evening's celebration. It was, he said, an important speech, because the Captain would be there at the party and he wanted to thank him for navigating the ship on her very first voyage. And he also wanted to thank his special guests and all the other first-class passengers for coming.

'But we should be thanking you!' said Connie.

'It doesn't work that way, Connie,' said Mr Bamberger ruefully. 'When you own a shipping line the most important thing is to keep your passengers happy. You want them to return for another voyage!'

However, it had struck Connie during tea in the first-class lounge that Mr Bamberger's guests didn't look happy at all as they nibbled their cucumber sandwiches and eclairs. They were solemn-faced and silent, still affected by Biffer Smith's outburst on deck that morning.

It was light outside the long windows, but since luncheon a white haze had sunk low over the sea, blurring the line of the horizon and hiding the sun. It had cast an eerie glow over the linen tablecloths and the pale faces of those seated around the little tables.

'Connie, shouldn't you be getting ready, too?' said Ida.

On the sofa in their stateroom Connie jumped guiltily. At her feet lay the jumble of her costume for the evening; she hadn't given it a glance yet.

'In a minute,' she said. Something had appeared in her mind's eye. Something significant. A little picture of the first morning. Had she been missing clues all along? They were there, a whole chain of them from the very first day, and now at last they were beginning to make sense. Her brain worked furiously.

Ida twirled in front of her, long green skirts shimmering, fair hair drifting down her back under its shell coronet. The scales on her mermaid tail sparkled.

'How do I look?' She smiled expectantly.

Connie examined her. 'Shouldn't your face and hands be green?'

'Oh.' Ida's face fell. 'Do you think so?'

'Well, Neptune's wife isn't human. She's a sea goddess.'

Ida looked worried. 'But I'm not sure Arthur would like me with a green face.' She brightened. 'Could I have green eyelids instead?'

'That might do, I suppose.'

'Then be a dear, Connie, and run along to Radmilla's stateroom and ask if I can borrow some green grease paint.'

'Can't you go?' Connie said, a little grumpily. While they had been talking she had been piecing together various clues – at least she thought they were clues. They might simply be false ones – red herrings. She needed time to think.

'But I don't want anyone to see me until I'm quite

ready and I might bump into Arthur. Please, darling Connie.'

Connie, like Arthur, could never resist Ida when she was at her most wheedling. She went along to Radmilla's stateroom, her mind whirring.

'Vat is it?' Radmilla shouted angrily through the shut door. 'I am zinking about my performance!'

Connie explained about Ida's predicament and eventually was let in.

A glittering white tutu, with feathers cleverly woven into the bodice and skirt, was hanging on the cupboard door, waiting for its occupant. The dressing-table was laden with sticks of theatrical grease paint and two pristine white ballet shoes with wide satin ribbons lay on the bed. Connie, distracted for a moment, cast a wistful glance at them. But no, she was going to be an anthropologist.

Radmilla herself was wearing a claret-coloured silk dressing-gown, with a Chinese dragon prowling over the back. Her face was bare of make-up and her black hair was down around her startlingly pale face. She looked younger and more vulnerable than Connie had ever seen her, though her frown was fierce.

'Hurry up! I must rehearse before tonight. Here!' She thrust her vanity case at Connie.

Connie took out a dark green stick with sparkles. 'Ida will be very grateful,' she said meekly.

On her way out she paused. 'You've never missed anything from this case, have you? An empty glass phial, for instance?'

Radmilla shook her head so furiously that strands of her hair flew like snakes around it. '*Nyet!* Now get out!'

Connie retreated and went thoughtfully back down the passage.

Ida seized on the green grease paint with delight and by the time Arthur appeared, looking most imposing in his Neptune costume, her eyelids were a startling seaweed green. At Connie's suggestion she had also smeared it on her mouth and covered her fair eyebrows.

Arthur seemed a little unnerved as he stood in the doorway of their stateroom, gazing at Ida with her sparkling green lips.

'I say, dearest, you look rather unhealthy – unearthly, I mean!'

Ida frowned uncertainly. 'That's what I'm meant to look, isn't it?'

'She's a creature of myth, Arthur,' said Connie sternly. 'Of course she's got to look unearthly. Put some on, yourself.' She held out the stick of grease paint in invitation.

He backed away. 'Thank you, Connie, but Ida looks beautiful whereas I'll look a complete nincompoop.'

'That's what I'm going to look,' said Connie glumly, as she surveyed her costume on the floor. The hatbox seemed to have lost its shape a little and now didn't look altogether convincing as the head of an exotic sea creature.

'Shall we help you into it, old thing?' said Arthur.

Connie shook her head.

Ida blew her a kiss that left the tips of her fingers green too, tucked her arm into Arthur's so that he had green fingerprints on his cloak, and then they were gone.

Connie pulled on Arthur's old shirt, pinned on the scarves, then looked disconsolately in the long mirror. She reached for her hairbrush and hesitated. There wasn't much point in brushing her hair if she was going to wear a headdress. She squinted sideways at one of her ringlets. The curl was coming out but no one would see.

It was then she realised what had been nagging at her. Of course – *of course!* She put the hairbrush down, stood for a moment deep in thought and then rushed to the door, her costume flapping about her.

She knew who would be able to answer her question. She couldn't ask Mr Bamberger – he might be hurt and bewildered by it – but there was somebody else.

Biffer Smith opened his door at once when she knocked. She was thrown for a moment to see that he didn't look like Biffer Smith at all.

They both stared at each other in astonishment: Biffer Smith, his face shadowed by an enormous Stetson hat, in rolled-up shirt-sleeves and a cowhide waistcoat; Connie, in her exotic sea creature costume minus the hatbox.

'Are you going as Wee Willie Winkie?' demanded Biffer.

'Are you going as a cowboy?' said Connie, without answering his question. To be compared to a nursery rhyme character in a nightshirt was an insult best ignored.

'Not any cowboy. Buffalo Bill, pioneer of the Wild West!' His eyes narrowed. 'What do you want?'

Connie lowered her voice. People were passing them on their way to the party.

Door and Veer looking glamorous and rather shocking in their squaws' costumes, which enabled them to display daring glimpses of bare arms and legs. Cornelia Cartmell was attired as Queen Victoria, like a black paper parcel, advancing with royal gait up the passage, accompanied by Muriel Pope, who looked much as she always did in the evenings, in droopy jacket and equally droopy long skirt. Hiram Fink, dressed, Connie guessed, as the great transatlantic passenger, Charles Dickens, with a leather-bound book and quill-pen in one hand; he tipped his top hat to Connie with the other as he passed.

He was followed by Louie Leblank, a somewhat elderly and unfit fur trapper, in boots and a leather jerkin, his white face almost hidden beneath an enormous beaver hat with a moth-eaten tail he had to keep flipping out of the way of his mouth.

Connie took a deep breath.

'I need to ask you a question, Mr Smith,' she whispered. 'It's awfully important. You could say, *vital*.'

'Now is not the most convenient time, even for a vital question.' Biffer Smith saw Connie's face and his journalist's curiosity took over. 'Hurry up, then,' he said grudgingly. 'And speak louder, girl! Age is catching up with me.'

Connie had the answer she needed from Biffer Smith.

It hadn't been a surprise; it only confirmed what she had been beginning to suspect. Now she knew the answer, she knew everything. There was only one person, one person alone, who was the final intended victim of the voyage.

She needed to warn Mr Bamberger of what might happen. The trouble was she didn't know if she had lots of time – or none at all. She needed to get to the party and observe everything very carefully indeed.

Back in her stateroom she crammed on the hatbox. She could only see what she looked like in sections in the mirror because Arthur had made the eye slits too small. She looked peculiar rather than exotic, but then there were much more important things than appearance at stake now.

She felt her way to the door and was out in the passage.

It seemed very quiet suddenly, but perhaps that was only because most of the passengers had already gone to the party – or perhaps the cardboard of the hatbox was muffling all sound. It was dark inside it too, and rather stuffy, and being inside a hatbox was so muddling that she began to think she had turned the wrong way.

She blundered along, touching the wall on her left-hand side to guide her. She needed to go to Mr Bamberger's stateroom first, to warn him, and when she raised the hatbox, she saw that she was indeed at the bend in the passage and had almost reached his door.

She thumped on it with her fist, just in case he was so immersed in preparing his speech that he couldn't hear a polite knock.

'Mr Bamberger! It's me, Connie. I've got something urgent to tell you!'

There was no answer, so she tried again. Then she turned the door handle. The door didn't budge. He must have already gone to the party. There was no time to lose!

Connie's headdress bumped down into place and she hurried around the bend, still touching the walls for guidance. She must be nearing the stewards' room. Then she would head for the lift.

She couldn't go as quickly as she wanted because Arthur's shirt was rather too long and she didn't want to trip. The cardboard in front of her mouth was getting a little damp. She still couldn't see very much. She tried to lift the hatbox off entirely, but it had become snagged in her hair. When she wiggled it about, it caught on the back of her costume.

Was that someone behind her? Or her heart thumping in her ears?

She hesitated, stopped blindly for a moment. There was a sudden violent push on her back, between her shoulder blades. She stumbled forward in shock. There was another even stronger push and she collapsed, sightless and disorientated, on to a hard floor.

Somewhere, a door shut behind her and a key turned in the lock.

23

For a moment or two, Connie lay still. She thought her heart had stopped in shock. But she wasn't hurt, she discovered, when after a bit she moved a little. And her heart seemed to be beating again, though rather rapidly.

But where was she?

There was a dead-feeling silence around her. She knew she must be in some enclosed space. Cautiously, she drew herself up on to all fours. She breathed in cardboard and suffocating thick darkness. She sat back gingerly.

The hatbox was pressing against her nose. It had been dented by her fall but still tugged painfully on her hair. She wrenched it off.

Without it, the darkness seemed just as dense and smelled disgustingly of chemicals and dust. Her nostrils prickled with it. A little while in here and there would be no air left to breathe. It was a place for brooms and bottles of bleach – definitely not for human girls. No wonder Mrs Cartmell had panicked.

And now she, Connie, was locked in the utility room and for her there would be no rescuers. All the passengers had gone to the party and the stewards and bellboys before them.

She reached out an arm. She could feel the door behind her, although she couldn't see it. There was no door handle this side but her fingers explored and found the outline of a keyhole. That was no good without a key. She gave the door a trial push. Then a stronger one. It didn't shift.

She sat back. All she could do was wait until everyone started coming back from the party and then bang on the door.

But by then murder would have been committed – probably at the party: she knew that now, almost certainly. She alone knew who the murderer was; only she knew why.

Meanwhile, she should try to breathe as little as possible without actually expiring. The air was so foul that she thought she might be sick. There was something else in it that she almost recognised but it was overlaid with sharp and acrid smells and peppery, clogging dust.

Then in the silence something moved.

It made too much noise to be a mouse or a rat. It was a human sound, a heavy shuffle, as if someone was shifting position, possibly preparing to attack her.

Connie held her breath and sat rock still. In such a confined space she would have no chance of escape. Her heart thumped horribly and she swallowed a moan. She listened hard but whoever it was must be listening too, because now there was no sound at all.

She had to breathe and so, evidently, did the other person. They both drew a huge breath at the same time and then, disastrously, Connie coughed on her lungful of foul air.

There was the sudden flare of a match. In the yellow light a pair of eyes gleamed at her from a face that was as frightened as her own must be and that had quite lost its usual jaunty look.

'*Bobby!*' said Connie.

'Blooming heck, it's you!' He blew out the match before it burned his fingers. 'It didn't half give me a fright when you fell in. I could just make out this monster shape against the light.'

'It's my costume.' Connie's heart slowed a little. No assailant but she was still locked in, even if she had a companion in adversity.

'What on earth are you doing in here, mate? Looking for clues?'

'No,' said Connie crossly. 'I was pushed in.' She rubbed her back, which still felt sore. 'Did you see who it was?'

'Couldn't see a sausage. Just your head blocking the light.'

'What are *you* doing in here? Did you get pushed in, too?'

'I came to fetch a fag.'

'A cigarette? In here?'

'I hide 'em in here when I've got 'em. Mr Bamberger forbids us bellboys to smoke, see? If I'm lucky, sometimes my pal down in the boiler rooms slips me a couple.'

'Oh.' So that was what he'd been doing the previous evening! She started as he gripped her ankle. 'But don't tell on me, will you? I'll be in right trouble.'

'Of course not! But we're in trouble now, Bobby! Whoever it was, locked the door!'

'Peasy.' He sounded pleased with himself. 'Got a key, haven't I? Pinched it from the stewards' room. Come to think of it, the spare was missing. Whoever pushed you in must have taken it.'

'Then let's get out of this hateful place! I've got to stop a murder!'

'Blimey, girl! Righto, hang on a sec. Need some light. Can you light a match?'

'Of course,' said Connie indignantly, but when Bobby passed her the box in the darkness she found that her hands were trembling.

At last the match flared and in its shaky light Bobby turned the key. Connie blew out the smouldering stub and as the door gave, they pushed hard and shot out together on to the passage floor in a tangle of limbs.

They lay sprawled for some moments, blinking at one another in relief in the bright light.

'My, that's a rum get-up,' said Bobby at last, staring at Connie's costume. 'What are you going as?'

'It's actually what you're going as,' said Connie, untangling her legs and dusting herself down with hands that had now stopped trembling. 'I've got an A1 idea!'

She reached back into the utility room and brought out her battered headdress. There was still time to prevent a tragedy if Bobby would pull himself together!

A deeply suspicious look had come over his face. 'What do you mean?'

'I'll show you,' said Connie. She marched along to the stewards' room.

'Hey!' said Bobby in alarm. 'You can't go in there!'

'Why not? They've all gone to the party and we need somewhere private to lay our plans.'

'What plans? I haven't any plans!'

'I've enough for both of us. Now get up! There's no time to lose!'

'Turn your back and don't look!' ordered Connie.

'Don't you look either!' retorted Bobby.

They were standing in the deserted stewards' room, in a stale fug of tobacco and beer. Empty chairs watched them as they discarded their outer clothes, Connie with relief, Bobby with extreme reluctance. It had taken a while to persuade him, precious moments that Connie knew she needed desperately.

'Bobby!' she had said at last in exasperation, when he hadn't even taken off his shoes. 'If murder takes place, you will lose your job! There will be a terrible scandal and no one will want to sail on the *Princess May* ever again!'

'I'll lose my job anyway, if they find out I've lent my

uniform to a passenger!' said Bobby glumly, but he took off his jacket, which was at least a start.

'You wait. If my hunch works out, then they'll be thanking us!'

The trouble was, Connie wasn't absolutely sure it would work out. She tried to stop herself from having doubtful thoughts. 'You want to do this for Mr Bamberger, don't you?'

Bobby's expression lightened. 'Oh, yeah! Mr Bamberger's been everything to me! He's a real gent. When I played around during my training and the head steward wanted to chuck me out, Mr Bamberger said he'd give me another chance. I'd do anything for him.'

'Well, then. You've got to do this.'

Bobby climbed out of his trousers. Connie didn't mean to look but his legs did look so very thin and white that she felt a pang. The Sisters of Hope orphanage had never fed its children properly. It seemed even more important to prevent murder on the *Princess May*, so that she could ensure that Bobby always had enough to eat in the future.

'I feel a right ass in this get-up,' Bobby said sulkily.

Connie refrained from saying that he looked it too. 'The thing is, we need people to believe you're me and

I'm you. It doesn't matter if you look silly or not.'

'Hmm.' Bobby surveyed her from head to foot. His uniform, which he was outgrowing fast, was a remarkably good fit on her. His black shoes were a little big and the shoulders of his red jacket a little empty at the sleeve seams, but otherwise Connie was positive she looked every inch a bellboy.

She grinned. 'I've never worn trousers before!'

She felt an extraordinary freedom and power. What a relief not to have to bother with woollen stockings and a pinafore that wrapped itself around your knees! If you wore trousers, you could stride through the world like a prince and people would listen to you.

'You look like a girl dressed as a boy,' said Bobby grumpily.

'Wait!' said Connie. She snatched up his pill-box hat, swept her hair up and jammed the hat over it, beaming at him triumphantly. He tilted the hat to one side a little, adjusted the strap under her chin and nodded.

'You'll do, mate. You don't look like me, though.'

'That doesn't matter,' said Connie patiently. 'I just need to look like a bellboy – any bellboy.'

'They'll have dimmed the lights, I daresay. So I have to go dressed in this lot? Your shoes are too small!

Me in girls' slippers – hope the lads don't guess. Can't see how this is going to help Mr Bamberger.'

Connie seized up the hatbox. She jammed it on Bobby's head before he could protest any more. 'You're a brick, Bobby! I knew I could rely on you. You won't need to say anything, just stay in the background.'

A mumble came from the hatbox. Connie thought she could make out, 'But I can't see!'

There was no time for sympathy. 'I'll be your eyes, Bobby. Leave everything to me. Now, come on!'

24

Bobby shuffled along in Connie's wake. 'I can't see nothing!' he mumbled, through cardboard.

'Then take my hand.'

'I'm not taking a blooming girl's hand, even if you are first-class!'

She grabbed his, all the same. 'Don't make such a silly fuss! We've got to get there!'

And somehow they did, Connie half dragging Bobby along as he lurched and stumbled.

Passengers they overtook looked at Connie approvingly. 'How perfectly sweet, darling,' one lady murmured to her male companion, as they advanced along rather more decorously. 'A bellboy helping a child to the party – gracious, what can it be going as?'

'An exotic sea creature!' grunted Bobby, but they had already left them behind.

'Do we have to go so fast?' Connie made out

through the hatbox. 'These slippers ain't great for speed!'

'I told you,' she hissed. 'It'll be murder on the *Princess May* unless I get there in time!'

The ballroom was brightly lit, the chandeliers gleaming on the elaborate costumes of the passengers. Red Indians arrayed in glossy feathers and fringed skirts and cowboys with lassooes mingled with sailors, morris-dancers, guards in red jackets and busbies, policemen, doctors and nurses. There were several Neptunes with their consorts, but none, Connie noted, as she spotted them holding court amongst the throng, quite as splendid and regal as Arthur and Ida, even though Ida's face was rather smeary with green grease paint by now.

The light sparkled like liquid gold on the glasses of champagne the guests held to their lips. At the moment the stage, where the orchestra usually played, was empty, except for a piano, waiting for Arthur to play for Radmilla later.

Radmilla herself lurked in a corner, wearing her claret dragon robe over ballet tights and looking stormy and superior, her dark eyes dramatically made up. Mrs Pope had retreated with her and was offering her champagne and possibly some words of eager and sympathetic encouragement, which Connie couldn't hear above the hubbub.

Through his eye slits Bobby spotted the canapés. They were arranged on silver salvers along the linen-covered tables that ran the length of the room: smoked oysters, potted cheese on little biscuits, slices of hard-boiled egg in jellied aspic on little squares of toast.

'Food!' came the muffled whisper. 'I ain't half hungry!'

'Later!' Connie said, struggling to wipe away the memory of his thin legs. 'Anyway, you can't eat through cardboard!'

A moan came from inside the hatbox.

'There you are at last, Connie!' said Ida and she grabbed Bobby, while Connie swept up a dinner menu from a table and hid her face behind it.

'Come and meet the Comtesse. You will speak French to her, won't you? I haven't a clue what she's saying! You've got to help Arthur out.'

'I can't,' growled Bobby.

'What's that, darling?'

'I can't speak French!'

''Course you can! All those years with Miss Poots. Have you got a sore throat? You sound most peculiar.'

'I say, Connie,' said Arthur to Bobby in a puzzled

way. 'That extra sleep last night must have done you good! You've grown!'

'*Ah, voilà! La petite cousine! Je suis enchanté de te rencontrer!*' An elegant lady in diamond tiara and satin opera cape stretched out a white hand to shake Bobby's, noticed his still bore the dust of the utility room and withdrew hers hastily. She inspected the sea creature's costume with curiosity.

'*C'est intéressant. Quel est ce déguisement, je prie? C'est ingénieux mais tres étrange.*' What is your costume? It is ingenious but very strange.

'Ta, I'm sure,' said Bobby, mistaking the bafflement in her voice for praise.

'*Comment?* You wish for tea, *mon enfant?*'

Connie, who was lurking behind Bobby, trying to hide her face from Ida, whispered in his ear, 'Say *merci, Madame*, not "ta".'

'Mercy, madam,' growled Bobby. He turned to Connie. 'Why should I be asking her for mercy? Anyway, I don't want tea!'

'Stop talking,' hissed Connie. 'Or they'll smell a rat!'

An expression of alarm crossed the French lady's face. '*Y-a-t-il un rat?*' she asked loudly. Ida, who had been used to rats as well as mice in her previous life at the orphanage, didn't blanch.

Connie tried to shake her head at the French lady and look reassuring without Ida or Arthur noticing.

'No rats on this ship, ma'am, and that's a fact,' said Bobby gruffly but only Connie heard.

'Be quiet!' she whispered furiously.

It was time to go.

Ida turned. 'Connie?' she said in bewilderment to Connie's back, as she disappeared with alacrity into the crowd. 'Goodness, Arthur, did you see that bellboy? He looks awfully like our Connie!'

'He has gone to fetch the tea, I think,' said the French lady. 'And to do something about the smell of rat, *peut-être.*' She wrinkled her nose. 'Though I smell only *Jicky de Guerlain*. Exquisite.'

Ida beamed complacently and forgot all about the mysterious bellboy, who was by now safely the other side of the room.

'How's tricks, Connie?' squeaked Elmer, popping up at Connie's elbow. He was dressed as an Indian prince, in a turban held together precariously by a large fake emerald brooch, and a satin coat that was rather too large for him.

'I'm meant to be a bellboy, not Connie, you duffer!' Connie said crossly, looking around in case anyone had heard.

'I can see that.' He clutched his turban, which had a tendency to topple. 'Swell costume! Looks like the real thing.'

'It is the real thing,' said Connie. 'Look, can you help me? It's really important.'

He crammed his turban down more securely, looking pleased. 'Sure I can!'

'I want you to go and talk to that – thing – that's talking to Ida.' She tried to point through the crowd, but people were annoyingly tall.

Elmer stood on the tips of his green embroidered slippers. 'The hatbox, you mean?'

'It didn't look like a hatbox when we first decorated it,' said Connie defensively. 'It's had a bad time since. Underneath it is Bobby the bellboy, only he's meant to be me.'

'OK,' said Elmer, confused and cautious.

'I want you to take him off somewhere so Ida doesn't suspect. It's so I can get on with watching someone.'

Elmer looked a little disappointed in his task. 'Is that all? Are you about to unmask the joker?'

'The joker isn't joking at all,' said Connie, 'but deadly serious. I'm talking about murder, Elmer!'

'Hey, you, bellboy!' said a steward's voice in Connie's ear. 'Conversing with passengers! I could report you!' To Elmer he said, 'I do apologise, young sir.'

Elmer's face was still taken aback by Connie's announcement but he pulled himself together with remarkable aplomb. 'It's OK, steward,' he said, and managed not to squeak. 'I was asking this young lady – gentleman, I mean – a question about the timing of dinner tonight.'

'Nine o'clock, sir,' said the steward but he cast a stern eye at Connie. 'I need you to help with trays. Come with me, lad!'

He crooked a sharp finger at Connie and she was forced to follow. She cast a hopeless look back at Elmer. This was the last thing she wanted. She needed to be free to watch and wait.

In fact, having a trayload of full glasses turned out to be an advantage.

It was so dreadfully heavy at first that she almost sank beneath its weight but once she had offloaded a few glasses on to a handy table, it was much more manageable. Then she could weave between the partying passengers, avoiding Mr Bamberger's guests who would know her face but keeping an eye on them all the time, while looking busy and dutiful.

Passengers, clustered in groups, took the full glasses from her tray and replaced them with their empty ones without even looking at her, while they engaged in vivacious conversation or the occasional shriek of laughter beneath their elaborate headdresses. No one thanked her.

How rude! But how fortunate, since Connie could feel some long wisps of hair escaping from beneath her pill-box hat and curling round her chin. She didn't have any hands to spare to tuck them away, so she pressed on grimly and, she hoped, invisibly, through the crowd.

Where was Mr Bamberger?

As she wondered, he appeared on the stage, accompanied by Captain Boniface. Louie Leblank bounded on behind them, looking down on the guests with an all-embracing smile. The captain looked dazzlingly handsome in his immaculate white suit and brass buttons; Mr Bamberger, in his usual evening dress of white tie and tails, a little tighter now than at the start of the voyage, looked his benign self, if embarrassed to be the focus of attention.

Louie Leblank's fur hat was rather too warm and his pallid face gleamed with sweat under the lights.

However, his self-confidence didn't falter as he held up his hand for silence. He flicked the tail of his beaver hat out of the way of his mouth; the tip looked a little sticky already.

'Ladies and gentleman, as your master of entertainment, it is my pleasure to present to you our valiant Captain, who has brought us safely across the ocean through storm and perilous seas.'

Captain Boniface bowed graciously. Louie Leblank gestured at Mr Bamberger. 'And, of course, the man without whom none of us would be here, for indeed, there would be no ship to sail in – Mr Waldo Bamberger!'

Guests and first-class passengers broke into enthusiastic clapping and clustered closer to the stage. Connie, her tray wobbling dangerously, was swept forward, her view blocked by a wall of backs. It was vital that she could see.

'Excuse me, sir. Excuse me, madam,' she muttered. Around her, women melted away, terrified that champagne would be spilled on their dresses. The men she simply dug in the ribs with her tray.

Surprisingly, soon she found she could edge her way right to the front, emerging by the steps that led up to the stage. She slipped along to the nearest corner, where Radmilla and Muriel Pope had now been joined by Biffer Smith and Hiram Fink, and laid her tray down on the table thankfully.

Out of the corner of her eye she could see Queen Victoria and the Indian prince standing close together: it struck her that Elmer was almost as tall as his mother when he stood up properly. He had his arm around her protectively and she was smiling at him. He caught Connie's glance, looked over and winked.

No one else paid her any attention: they were all gazing up at Mr Bamberger, who was well into his speech. Biffer Smith was scribbling furiously in his notebook; Muriel Pope was staring at him intently, as if she did not wish to miss a word; Radmilla was biting her lip and frowning as she waited for her own performance to come, and Hiram Fink's expression was inscrutable, as it always was.

'… and so we have an extra cause for celebration tonight. Not only is this her maiden voyage, the first of many, for the *Princess May*, but I am delighted to tell you that it looks as if we shall win the Blue Riband tomorrow as we arrive in New York! To date we have broken the record for speed across the Atlantic. Two firsts, ladies and gentlemen! All thanks to our Captain, of course –' here Boniface shook his head modestly '– and to his hard-working crew, and to the beautiful design of this ship which did not lose speed, even during heavy weather. So let us drink a toast to the *Princess May* and all who sail in her! You, my dear passengers!'

There was rapturous applause and a terrific clinking of glasses, led by Mr Bamberger's guests who grouped about the bottom of the steps as he descended.

Muriel Pope pressed forward, eager to please as always. 'Oh, you haven't a drink yourself, dear Mr Bamberger! Let me get you one!'

'How kind, Mrs Pope,' said Mr Bamberger, smiling. 'Yeah, I sure feel like celebrating!'

Connie took a full glass from her tray and held it out to Mrs Pope.

'Can't you see that one has a smear on it, bellboy?' whispered Mrs Pope. 'Remove it and have it washed. I'll get one myself!'

Connie examined the glass, but she knew it was perfectly clean. And so did Mrs Pope.

No one saw as Mrs Pope bent over the few full glasses left on the tray. No one, except Connie. Everyone was calling up to Mr Bamberger with congratulations. Someone even broke into a rousing rendition of 'For he's a jolly good fellow!'

Connie took a few steps away with the offending glass and looked back. No one saw Muriel Pope, alone at the table, take a small white paper package from her reticule and pour its contents into a full glass of champagne. No one, except Connie. No one except Connie saw her stir it with a darning needle so that the stiff mass of crushed sleeping pills melted in the golden liquid.

Muriel Pope advanced towards Mr Bamberger with the glass held aloft and a shy smile on her lips. She reached up to Mr Bamberger with the glass as he came down the steps. 'You deserve a drink, Mr Bamberger. You really do – *deserve* – it.'

'Thank you, Mrs Pope,' said Mr Bamberger, a little astonished by such effusiveness from the normally quiet woman, and he took the glass gratefully.

'I'll say he does,' said Louie Leblank on the steps behind him and he gave the table a hopeful look to check whether any full glasses remained. 'Wouldn't mind one myself, not that poor little me deserves it, of course.'

Mr Bamberger reached the bottom of the steps, raised his glass and looked around as if to toast everyone present. Then he put it to his lips.

'*No!*' shouted Connie.

She tore the few steps back, cannoning between Biffer Smith and Hiram Fink, and dashed the glass from Mr Bamberger's hand.

It fell, shattering into shards that shot out over the floor. The spilled champagne stayed in a thick and oddly repellent puddle by the steps. By it Bobby's pill-box hat lay on its side, fallen from Connie's head as she ran.

People near the stage drew in their breath at such affrontery. There was a shocked silence.

'Connie!' exclaimed Mr Bamberger, in bewilderment.

'Connie!' cried Ida, who had come up to the stage steps with Arthur and Bobby in tow, the latter still in disguise. She turned in astonishment and rapped on the hatbox. 'Come out, whoever you are!'

'Connie!' hissed Muriel Pope. There was a terrifying madness in her eyes.

She lunged at Connie with the long darning needle but before she could reach her, Biffer Smith had grabbed her arm. The needle fell away uselessly and stuck in the floor.

'Oh, no, Mrs Pope,' said Connie firmly, even if she was a little breathless. 'It's not me you want to kill, is it? It's Mr Bamberger. But how could murdering him bring back your drowned son? You surely don't want to hang for murder, do you, Mrs Pope?'

Muriel Pope gasped at her, wildness in her face. Around the table and on the stage steps everyone remained absolutely still, rigid with horror.

'You didn't really want to kill Mr Bamberger, anyway, did you?' Connie went on, her voice so soft and unalarming that only those nearest her could hear it. 'If your other scheme had worked – the chain of alarming events you had planned to frighten and even endanger his guests – then Mr Bamberger's reputation would have been ruined and no one would have wanted to sail on his new ship ever again. That was what you wanted at the beginning, wasn't it? You weren't intending to kill him then. But that scheme failed, didn't it?'

Mrs Pope nodded. Tears began to stream down her face. She dashed them away savagely and spat out, 'It was then I decided he deserved to die!'

'But Mr Bamberger wasn't to blame for your son's death,' Connie said gently. 'No one was. You know that in your heart of hearts. It was a tragic accident, that was all.'

'*All?* What can you, a child, know about losing a son? He was everything to me – everything! He was my life!'

With a terrible moan Muriel Pope wrenched herself away from Biffer Smith's hold and fell on the floor, weeping bitterly.

When the security officers arrived, she began to writhe and shout in their grip, words which scarcely had any meaning. In the struggle her grey-streaked wig came off and beneath it she was revealed as a young woman still, perhaps in her mid-thirties. But the thwarted rage in her eyes as she was dragged away was age-old, a mother's desire for revenge on a man she would always believe had been the cause of her son's death.

Ida rushed up to Connie and threw her arms tight around her. Arthur, close behind, put his arm around Ida and his free hand on Connie's shoulder, so that they stood encircled in a warm, supportive little group.

Connie was glad of their comfort. She felt hollow inside, as if she had no feelings of her own left. For the moment that was the only way she cope with the sight of Mrs Pope's bitter tears, even if they had been the tears of a would-be murderess.

Bobby tugged off the hatbox violently – it had become stuck once again – and released from its prison he caught sight of Connie with relief and darted over.

'Hey, mate! I couldn't see nothing! Did you save Mr Bamberger and unmask the murderer?'

The first part of his question was answered by the ample frame of Mr Bamberger close by, surrounded by anxious guests and clearly still very much alive – which more or less answered the second part, too.

His eyes widened. 'You did, didn't you! I never!'

'Bobby Sparrow! Whatever do you think you're wearing?' A steward appeared from nowhere. 'No matter – get that mess cleaned up at once!' He pointed at the sinister puddle still lying thickly at the bottom of the stage steps.

'It's evidence,' Connie murmured but she wasn't

heard, and Bobby trailed off in a flutter of scarves after
first rescuing his hat.

Then Connie found herself congratulated by all
those she had once thought possible suspects.

Hiram Fink pressed her hand, his face concerned,
as if he understood her confused feelings. Biffer Smith
nodded and grinned, as if he were acknowledging an
equal at last. Door and Veer's kohl-lined eyes grew
larger still. Mrs Cartmell was gracious but genuine.

'Lolla palooza!' said Elmer. 'Swell work, kiddo!'
He looked at Connie sideways. 'I did help a little,
didn't I?'

'Oh, yes!' said Connie. 'You gave me the first clue
but I didn't realise it at the time.'

'That's my boy!' said Mrs Cartmell proudly.

Only those nearest the stage had seen the drama of the
attempted murder of Mr Bamberger. The passengers
further back in the ballroom had had their view
blocked by others, just as Connie's had been earlier.
But they were aware that something had happened
and were immensely curious.

Mr Bamberger looked white and quite unlike his

usual ebullient self. It was hardly surprising, since he had just escaped death. So it remained to either the Captain or Louie Leblank to ensure that the evening's entertainment went on with as little fuss as possible.

Captain Boniface was nonplussed and speechless. Even his white coat seemed less stiffly starched. Never in his entire and extremely successful sailing career had he encountered a murderous passenger before.

So it was left to Louie Leblank to continue the ceremonies.

He grabbed a glass of champagne from the table, examined its contents with the utmost care, then downed it in one. When he ascended the steps to the stage, it was with a new spring in his step. This was his moment.

He flicked the somewhat slimy beaver tail away from his mouth and smiled down at the faces before him.

'Ladies and gentleman, if any of you have been in the least perturbed by anything untoward just now, let me assure you that all is well. One of Mr Bamberger's special guests – poor unfortunate lady – has been taken ill most unexpectedly and removed to a safe place in isolation, where she will be taken care of.' He hesitated. 'I trust.'

The passengers turned to each other with anxious, enquiring faces. 'Can it be catching? Isolation? What illness?'

Louie Leblank cleared his throat.

'Let me assure you all that murd— whatever this lady is suffering from is neither infectious nor contagious.

'So let us continue with the highlight of this evening. That is the performance by the celebrated ballerina, Miss Radmilla Oblomov, whom we are so honoured to have amongst Mr Bamberger's special guests. She is to perform the dance of *The Dying Swan*.' He caught Ida's glare and added, 'Mr Arthur Harker, the ship's popular pianist, will play Saint-Saëns's sublime music to accompany her.

'So, ladies and gentleman, if you would all wait five minutes, our wonderful stewards will bring out chairs for your comfort and prepare the room.'

Radmilla had slipped away into one of the two dressing rooms behind the stage. Arthur went off into the other to change into evening dress, since King Nepture playing for a dying swan would be somewhat inappropriate. Ida and Connie went to sit down together.

Mr Bamberger took the chair on Connie's other

side. He placed his large warm hand over her small cold one and squeezed it.

'My dearest Connie,' he said simply. 'How can I ever thank you? You saved my life. And I didn't take you seriously despite all your warnings – for which I am heartily sorry, honey.'

That was enough for Connie. She drank her glass of lemonade and felt better.

The ballroom darkened, Arthur played the opening bars and Radmilla came on in her shimmering white-feathered tutu. Dreamily she circled the stage. Then she began to dance.

She moved exquisitely, precise with her tiny toe movements and fluid with her arms, stretching them out like wings to the distant horizon of death as if she yearned to fly there, her eyes eloquent with tragedy. Caught up in the emotion of the dance, the audience forgot all about the passenger who had been taken ill during the evening's celebrations. They were in the presence of a great ballerina.

When it was over Radmilla was applauded rapturously and had to die again several times – for Connie had been right: it was a very short solo – before people were satisfied.

When at last the other passengers had departed for

dinner, Mr Bamberger's special guests lingered in an excited bunch around Connie's chair. Having witnessed everything, there was so much they wanted to know before they went to the dining saloon.

Mr Bamberger turned to her and said quietly, 'Connie, do you feel like telling everyone how it was you so miraculously spotted that Mrs Pope was behind all the mishaps on the *Princess May*?'

Connie nodded. 'But it wasn't a miracle at all,' she whispered into his ear. 'I really didn't know for certain until I talked to Biffer Smith!'

'Sit down, everyone,' said Louie Leblank, still in his role of master of ceremonies, holding up a hand. 'We shall go into dinner a little late this evening.' His duty done, he took off his fur hat with relief and laid it on the chair next to him, where it lay damply, like an overfed sleeping cat.

Bobby sidled in and sat down. He was still dressed in the lower half of an exotic sea creature, but was wearing his pill-box hat again. Such was the extraordinary atmosphere of the evening that everyone accepted his unusual appearance, even a watchful steward.

Connie stood up. She felt more confident that way: sitting down she was almost lost in her chair.

Everyone fell silent and waited, for there was something about the small upright figure, standing alone under the glitter of the chandeliers, that held their attention.

She took a deep breath and began.

26

'I didn't suspect Mrs Pope at all to begin with,' said Connie.

'She was the victim of the first nasty prank, when her life-preserver leaked oil. It had been contained in a phial used in the theatre, so I thought Radmilla might be behind it.

'But then,' Connie continued, avoiding Radmilla's flashing black eyes, 'Ramilla herself was a victim the following morning when I found that her deckchair had been damaged. It had been almost sawn through.'

'Ah, yes, I nearly broke my back!' said Radmilla, glaring around in case anyone dared disagree. No one did.

'There were others among us who had also been involved in the theatre, so might have had access to a glass phial. For a while I suspected Miss Devine and Miss Vane.' Connie tactfully avoided mentioning

Louie Leblank.

'Meanwhile, the disturbing events went on. During the first night Mrs Pope said she had heard someone tramping up and down outside her cabin as if they were wearing sea boots. She said she thought it was the ghost of the drowned boy. My cousin Ida had seen a ghostly figure in yellow workman's overalls that night, too, and so did I. Rumours began to spread, just as Mrs Pope hoped they would.

'Oil was spilled outside Mrs Cartmell's stateroom. It was the same oil that had been in Mrs Pope's life-preserver because I took samples.

'Several of us saw the spectre in yellow overalls again, including Miss Devine, so I had to stop suspecting her.'

'Thank you, Connie, I'm sure,' said Door huffily, but was hushed by everyone.

'Mr Smith had pages torn from his notebook. He said they were a description of the conversation at dinner the first night. That was when the drowned boy was mentioned.

'Someone tried to push Mrs Cartmell overboard. Shortly afterwards she was shut into the utility room by a figure wearing yellow overalls. Then Mrs Pope thought she saw an albatross, a bird of ill omen, which frightened some people even more, especially when we sailed into a storm.'

Connie paused for breath and looked around at the watching faces.

'We remember the sequence of events all too well,' said Hiram Fink grimly. 'But how did you work out who was behind it all, Connie?'

'Mr Bamberger thought it was someone playing a series of pranks,' said Connie and Mr Bamberger shook his head ruefully.

'He wasn't always there when these things happened; he didn't realise how serious they were and how much they could harm him if the story got out and people never wanted to sail on the *Princess May* again. After all, a prominent journalist was travelling with us and the accidents always involved Mr Bamberger's own guests, the ones well known enough to influence people afterwards.

'But I didn't realise who was behind it for a long time. Some of us –' Connie looked around again slowly, passing over the faces of those she had once thought might be the culprit '– seemed to have a strong motive.'

A murmur of protest arose, quashed by Hiram Fink raising a hand.

'I even suspected Mr Fink himself at one stage,' said Connie demurely and there was laughter. She waited until it had died away and her audience was listening attentively again.

'Meanwhile, I couldn't work out whether Mr Smith was on Mr Bamberger's side or not. He seemed to enjoy writing up all the things that were going wrong.'

'I'm a journalist, Connie,' said Biffer Smith, as everyone turned to stare accusingly at him. 'I try to report the truth.'

'And you needed a story, didn't you?'

Biffer Smith shifted uncomfortably. 'I thought these strange mishaps had become pretty serious and that someone's life could be at risk. I decided to write everything up in case it was needed as evidence. But I won't be publishing it, Waldo. For the sake of old times, eh? Just a report of the luxury on board and the voyage itself.' He looked at Connie through narrowed eyes, as if testing her. 'It means you won't get your name in the papers, young lady. What a story it would make, eh?'

Connie ignored him and went on firmly, 'As far as Mrs Pope was concerned, there were several clues pointing to her that I missed until I thought about it all later.

'I was put off by the fact that she had been the first victim. She had, of course, put the oil in a phial inside her own life-preserver and then taken the cap off. She pretended that she had heard ghostly sea boots outside her cabin to frighten people, but claimed that Mrs Cartmell in the adjoining stateroom wouldn't have heard them because she was a heavy sleeper. It was also an excellent way to obtain the sleeping pills from the ship's doctor that she would later try to use on Mr Bamberger.

'I think she thought of them as a last resort. She didn't mean to use them until everything else failed.

'And then she said she had seen an "albatross". Albatrosses are not known on this sea.' Elmer nodded vigorously. 'She made that up, too.

'Her disguise was excellent and she had been a professional actress in her past. Now she was playing the role of an elderly, genteel lady in shabby clothes, eager to please everyone and most of all her employer, Mrs Cartmell.

'We all thought Mrs Pope was elderly because her hair was greying and she was stooped – though she was actually a tall, strong woman – and because of her mannerisms. I noticed her young hands when she was knitting. Of course she wasn't old at all.

'It was Elmer the first morning who found the treasured lock of hair that had belonged to her son. I didn't realise it was a vital clue but he thought it might be, and he was right all along.'

Elmer tried to look modest.

'I should have known,' admitted Connie. 'People keep locks of hair that mean something to them. My aunt once gave her daughter Ida a locket with her own hair inside.'

Ida nodded; tears glistened suddenly in her eyes.

'Mrs Pope always carried a reticule and it was ideal for hiding anything from a saw to a pair of yellow overalls – they were probably a spare pair of her son's – let alone her knitting and mending. She told me she had come on deck early because she'd had a bad night, but it was because she knew she would be alone then and could tamper with Radmilla's deckchair undisturbed.

'She made two attempts to frighten her employer deliberately. She was in charge of keeping Mrs Cartmell's clothes and it was easy enough for her to loosen the veil on the hat that Mrs Cartmell wore on the afternoon she was pushed while on deck. It was also Mrs Pope who pushed Mrs Cartmell into the utility room. As a paid companion she accompanied her employer most of the time: she learned a lot about her as she followed her about.'

Connie looked over meaningfully at Cornelia Cartmell, who tightened her lips. As she trailed after Mrs Cartmell up and down the stairs to every deck, Mrs Pope must have suspected that Mrs Cartmell avoided lifts because she feared small, claustrophobic spaces.

'Tonight Muriel Pope's reticule hid the packet of crushed sleeping pills she put in Mr Bamberger's glass. She'd got rid of the oil by dropping the tin overboard; I saw her do it, but didn't realise what it was at the time.

'She shut me into the utility room tonight to keep me out of the way,' Connie went on. 'She was planning to put the sleeping pills in Mr Bamberger's glass at the party. She knew he would be present. It was her last chance. It would have been a long time before I was discovered. Mr Bamberger might have been dead by then.'

'Oh, Connie!' cried Ida.

'It was quite all right, actually,' said Connie. 'Bobby Sparrrow let me out. He kindly allowed me to wear his uniform to the party so I'd be disguised.'

'Oh, Bobby!' said Ida, and she kissed him gratefully

on the cheek. Bobby blushed with pleasure and settled back in his chair, heartily relieved that Connie hadn't given away the secret of his cigarette stash.

'How did Mrs Pope know you suspected her, though?' said Hiram Fink.

'She must have heard me asking Mr Smith for the name of the drowned boy. You always hear your own surname, even when there's other conversation going on. She was walking past with Mrs Cartmell when I was talking to Mr Smith.'

'Also –' Connie wondered how best to put it. 'She discovered me doing – research – about her.'

'Connie, you put yourself in terrible danger,' said Mr Bamberger. 'You might have been murdered yourself!'

Connie shook her head. 'Mrs Pope was set on revenge. I wasn't her target. She wasn't a child killer.'

'Dreadful woman!' exclaimed Mrs Cartmell. 'To think that I employed a murderess and slept next door to one, too!' She shuddered.

'She loved her son,' said Connie simply. 'He was all she had after her husband left her. When her son drowned she was left to live with the tragedy alone. I think it made her mad.'

27

It was later that evening. Dinner was over and most of Mr Bamberger's guests had either gone to dance or had retired for the evening in preparation for an early start on deck to watch New York come into view.

Connie sat with Mr Bamberger, Ida and Arthur and Hiram Fink in the quiet first-class dining saloon. Stewards hovered discreetly; Bobby Sparrow hovered too, back in his bellboy's uniform, catching her eye and grinning every now and then.

For dinner, Connie had reluctantly changed back into a dress. But, she thought, when I become an anthropologist, I shall wear trousers whenever I want! How splendidly useful they would be for striding over desert sands or hacking her way through jungle to investigate unknown tribes.

'I fear you are lost to accountancy,' said Hiram

Fink. 'I hadn't realised your investigative talents were quite so formidable.'

Cornelia Cartmell, accompanied by Elmer, was among the last to leave and had been unusually silent and subdued, as if she had been debating something momentous. She marched up to where Connie was sitting and held out her hand. Connie, bemused, stood up and took it.

'Miss Carew, I trust you and your cousin and her fiancé will accept dinner with me in my hotel during your stay in Manhattan.'

It was a magnificent gesture of thanks and acceptance. Connie was aware that next to her, Ida's mouth had dropped open. 'I know that Elmer would be glad to see you again,' added Mrs Cartmell, as if it had been Elmer's suggestion in the first place and nothing to do with her.

Elmer hesitated, then pecked Connie on the cheek, while his mother gazed at them benevolently. 'Maybe there'll be a mystery to solve in Manhattan!' he whispered.

Connie looked after them, as Elmer escorted his mother from the dining saloon. For a moment she wondered what it would be like to have a mother still. Love was the strongest emotion of all, she thought, but the bond between mother and child could become warped – the wrong kind of love – like Mrs Pope's. Mrs Cartmell's and Elmer's looked as if it were fast developing into the right kind.

'I've agreed that Hiram become a director of the Shining Seas shipping line, which means he'll part own it,' Mr Bamberger said quietly to Connie. 'What do you think of that?'

'I'm glad – he's A1 with money!'

Hiram Fink smiled down into his coffee cup.

'Now,' said Mr Bamberger, leaning back and taking a sip from his own cup. Over its rim his eyes met Connie's. 'I was most impressed to hear of this "research" of yours – the research you did on Muriel Pope. Was it the same kind of research you did on poor Mr Fink and possibly on several other of my guests as well?'

'Tell us how you found the evidence, you clever old thing,' nodded Arthur. 'Mrs Pope's stage name and what not.'

Connie bit her lip. She would have to own up to snooping in other passengers' staterooms.

'I imagine you had the help of young Mr Sparrow,' said Mr Bamberger. 'Your investigations certainly wouldn't have progressed very far without his assistance. How lucky that he held the *key* to all you needed!'

'It wasn't his fault!' said Connie quickly. 'I made him do it!'

'Do what, Connie?' said Arthur.

Ida put her hand to her mouth as she put two and two together. 'Oh, Connie!' Over the top of her fingers her eyes held laughter.

Connie looked from Ida to Mr Bamberger and Mr Fink and saw that they were smiling, too.

'Perhaps we'll keep your investigative methods quiet, Connie, seeing that you've just saved my life!' said Mr Bamberger.

'*I* want to know,' said Arthur, looking put out. 'After all, I was Connie's partner when she solved the mystery of Ida. We faced danger together, didn't we, Connie?'

Connie nodded. 'You were a spiffing partner, Arthur!'

Arthur looked mollified but still perplexed.

'I found an old theatre programme by accident,' Connie told him, 'and it turned out to be my most important piece of evidence. It was tucked into a Bible which had been a confirmation present to Mrs Pope's son. It fell on me from a table when the ship lurched. It was old but Mrs Pope had kept it as if it was something she treasured, like a memento. Perhaps it was the last time she performed.'

'But what were you doing on the floor?' said Arthur, more puzzled still.

'We were all falling over with the ship's motion that day, weren't we?' said Ida, with a giggle.

'The programme had Mrs Pope's name in it, you see,' explained Connie. 'Only she wasn't Mrs Pope then, she was Miss Mason. She had a baby boy, Wilfred, when she wasn't married. She married Mr Pope later. She said he left her afterwards. That was true, I think.'

'Poor Mrs Pope,' said Ida. 'So she lost a husband and a son.'

'People do,' said Arthur. 'It doesn't make them loony, though.'

'She won't hang or go to prison, will she?' Connie asked Mr Bamberger.

He shook his head. 'This will be kept very quiet. No one knows what exactly was in that glass except you, Connie. Her mental condition will be assessed and she'll receive medical help. I think they'll find that her state of mind is disturbed and she isn't responsible for her actions.'

At that moment the Captain entered. All the stewards stood to attention as he came over to their table and whispered something in Mr Bamberger's ear. For a moment Mr Bamberger's face fell, then he recovered.

'Early start tomorrow,' he said, as the captain left. 'Poor Captain Boniface will be up all night guiding us in, especially in this weather.'

But the ship seemed as steady as anything, Connie thought, as she watched the Captain's departing back. What a huge responsibility it was being the master of a ship with all those lives on board, especially when one of them turned out to be a murderer!

The Captain was halfway to the door when he stopped, as if he had remembered something. Then he turned smartly, clicked his toes together and saluted – not Mr Bamberger but Connie herself.

I didn't really deserve a salute, thought Connie later, as she sat in bed and looked at the mess of crossings-out and question marks in her notebook.

It had taken her ages to solve the mystery and she had suspected all the wrong people, even Mr Fink, who had turned out to be nice and not nasty at all. Suspecting Mrs Pope for being behind all the calamities on board, realising that they were leading up to a tragedy and that that tragedy might be the murder of Mr Bamberger, had been mostly due to curiosity, a little bit of intuition and a lot of luck. None seemed worthy of a would-be anthropologist.

But perhaps that was all scientists ever had – curiosity, intuition and luck. One day she would find out. In the meantime, she had worked it out in the end, in time to save Mr Bamberger and his ship.

'Aren't you going to turn your light out, Connie?' complained Ida, with an enormous yawn. 'We've got to get up at five! We must have some sleep if we're going to wave as we pass the Statue of Liberty!'

'Especially if there's bad weather in the night,' said Connie, but Ida's answering groan had turned into a snore.

However, when a short while later Connie was woken by the murmur of voices as passengers walked past their door, the ship still seemed to be moving smoothly over a flat sea – in fact, hardly moving at all. Somehow it was five o'clock already.

'Wake up, Ida! We've arrived!'

But they hadn't arrived and when she got out of

bed she could feel the faintest vibration under her toes; the engines were still running but much slower. That must mean they were almost at their destination and that the Captain was being very careful as he navigated the *Princess May* into harbour.

When she drew the curtain back to look out of their window it was as if another pane of glass had been fitted there: thick and opaque so that she couldn't see through it. For a moment she didn't understand, then Ida, rubbing her eyes sleepily behind her, said, 'Oh, no, it's fog! We shan't be able to see anything at all.'

'We must go on deck, just in case,' said Connie and she threw on her warmest clothes and laced up her deck shoes. Somehow she felt sure that the situation would be different outside and that the fog would suddenly lift, allowing them to see the skyscrapers and towers of downtown Manhattan as they steamed into harbour.

Bobby was hanging about outside their stateroom when they emerged, sliding from one roller-skate to the other.

'Just wanted to say cheerio till next time,' he said, looking bashful.

Ida hugged him so that he wobbled dangerously. 'Don't expect a tip from me this trip, Bobby Sparrow!'

she said. 'You led my little cousin into trouble, you did!'

'It was the other way round!' he protested, pretending to look aggrieved. 'She couldn't have done without me, anyhow.' He grinned at Connie. 'See you on the way back, mate! Let's hope there are no murderers on board, eh?'

'And you'll give me a go on your roller-skates?' said Connie. 'You promised! It's been rather too busy this time.'

'Cross me heart!' said Bobby, and he executed a perfect turn before he skated away.

Up on deck the fog seemed just as dense and even rather eerie.

Cold, disappointed passengers stood about, staring blindly into the cloying grey murk, trying to glimpse the outline of banks moving past. When the feeble glimmer of a light showed they would rush over to that side expectantly, only to discover that it illuminated nothing and had soon faded altogether, like a dying star.

Connie spotted the lone bulky figure of Mr Bamberger, well wrapped up in his dark overcoat, silhouetted against the fog. It was time to say goodbye and she couldn't help a pang at the thought they would have no more teatime talks together. Although Arthur would be playing again on the return voyage to Southampton, Mr Bamberger would be remaining in the New York offices of the shippine line, at least for a while.

'Well, Captain Boniface brought us through last night OK,' he said as she came up, with Ida and Arthur behind her. 'Nasty stuff, fog. A captain would rather face stormy seas than navigate into harbour with fog.'

'The *Princess May* won't win the Blue Riband now we're going so slowly, will she?' said Connie.

He shook his head. 'I knew it last night when the captain told me at dinner. Safety before speed, eh? But heck! It's only an honorary award at the moment. There's no trophy.'

'Oh,' said Connie. So perhaps it wasn't so very disappointing after all. She had imagined a gold statuette of the captain with a blue ribbon round his neck, sitting in pride of place in Mr Bamberger's offices.

'Anyway, there's always a next time,' said Mr Bamberger.

'Is there?' said Connie. There wouldn't be for them. She didn't think they would ever meet again.

She waited while Ida and Arthur thanked him for the voyage, but after they had gone it was difficult to know what to say. Mr Bamberger was making polite conversation because he didn't want to say goodbye either, Connie thought sadly. It was up to her.

She held out her hand. 'Goodbye, Mr Bamberger, and thank you for a ripping time.'

At once he took her chilly hand in his and held it between his gloved ones.

'I hope this is not goodbye, Connie. I rather wondered if I might take you out for tea at Fortnum's when I'm over.' He looked at her hopefully. 'It can get a little lonely when I'm by myself in London. I'd ask permission from your aunt, of course. Would it tempt you at all?'

'Of course it would! It would be absolutely A1, Mr Bamberger!' A thought struck Connie. Aunt Dorothea got lonely too. 'Would it be all right if I brought my aunt as well?'

'Swell idea, my dear.'

Connie skipped off to rejoin Ida and Arthur. Ida nudged her. 'I overheard that! Connie, are you matchmaking?'

'No,' said Connie innocently. But of course it

would be the most A1 thing in the whole world if two people she was so fond of fell in love – as good as Ida and Arthur.

They stood at the deck rail, close together for warmth, Connie sandwiched between them.

The wood was wet under Connie's hands. Her hair was soon lank with the damp and she could feel moisture dripping down from the brim of her hat on to her face and clothes. When she licked her lips she tasted not salt any longer but rain – earthy rain. Their temporary world of sea and spray had been left behind in the fog. Soon they would be shorebound again but in a completely new world.

Excitement stirred inside her. What thrilling opportunities did America hold?

She couldn't see any of the famous landmarks of Manhattan – but she knew they were there, waiting for her like a promise somewhere in the fog, as hidden to her at this moment as the next adventure the future would surely bring.

Author's Note

I was mulling over whether to include a ballet dancer among Mr Bamberger's guests in *The Ship of Spectres*, when I discovered that earlier the same summer of 1909 that the *Princess May* sets sail in my story, the great impresario, Sergei Diaghilev, had taken his company, the Ballets Russes, to Paris for its very first season. It was hugely successful and the Ballets Russes went on to become the most artistically creative and influential ballet company of the Twentieth century.

So my fictitious character, Radmilla Oblomov, could be a member of the company, I thought. But why would a Russian prima ballerina be making a transatlantic passage?

Then I found that Diaghilev had ambitions to tour his company to America – and finally did so in 1916. However, he was never able to travel with it because of his fear of water: he was terrified of death by drowning. So that's why Radmilla sails on the *Princess May*! She is an emissary sent by Diaghilev (though perhaps not an ideal one!) to talk to producers in New York because he is too frightened of sea travel to go there himself.

I also had an image of a roller-skating bell boy in my mind. How better to speed along the endless glossy passages of the *Princess May*? I didn't expect to find that the year 1909 was, in fact, the peak of a roller-skating craze ('rinking', as it was called) that gripped the Edwardians for a short period, with over 500 rinks opening and even a World Professional Roller-Skating Championship held in Britain that year!

When it came to the *Princess May*, I modelled her on a combination of the *Lusitania* (launched in 1906) and her sister ship, the *Mauretania* (1907), and the ill-fated *Titanic* (1912). The public rooms of these ships were designed and decorated magnificently in Edwardian taste and their cabins achieved a standard of luxury never seen on board before. The ships were driven by steam turbines, which were much quieter and faster than the old respricating engines, and meant they could travel at up to 25 knots across the North Atlantic. (The *Mauretania*, in fact, won the Blue Riband for twenty years running.) The only thing ships didn't have in those days were stabilisers – so in rough seas, you might have felt very sick indeed!